A FRACTURE IN SPACE

BY

CHRIS R SPENCER

"And pray that there's intelligent
life somewhere up in space,
'Cause there's bugger all down here on Earth."
-- Eric Idle

"We don't talk about love
We only wanna get drunk
And we are not allowed to spend
As we are told that this is the end"
-- Manic Street Preachers

Author's Note:

Without the influence of Douglas Noel Adams (1952-2001; Rest in Peace), this work would not have been possible. At first readthrough, a reader might think this is exclusively to do with the style and sense of humor. Whilst this is correct, it is only part of the story. The other part has to do with his lack of fondness for deadlines. So here we are, *an entire decade later.*

CHAPTER 1

STORMY BEGINNINGS PART 1

Once, there was Marwood.

The best, and most politically correct way to describe Marwood would be to say that he was an extrovert. The less politically inclined would say that he was a wild old bastard, with a slight tendency towards the eccentric side of life. Marwood was dependable when it came to personal discourse, when it involved a volume of alcohol that caused even the most seasoned (and the wealthiest of) drinkers to run away screaming when the bill finally arrived. He also dabbled a little in the drug world.

Well, dabbling would be a generous way of putting it, and you'd want to be generous with Marwood. He was incredibly charismatic. Some would say that he was like a character portrayed by Hugh Grant, except that you didn't want to punch him in the face for being so smug. Others would say that he could literally charm the paint off walls. These people were some of his nearest and dearest, and claimed to have seen this actually happen, and so you could see why dabbling would be a generous way of putting it. The jury at his trial all agreed amongst themselves that, as well as him being "not guilty" (because who could sentence a man with that kind of smile and those eyes to jail?), "dabbling" was the best way of putting it too. Marwood and his friend Wesley were charged with destruction of property when they decided, on a high note, to drive Marwood's Ford Mustang through a shopping mall on a Saturday afternoon. They were shouting "I'm coming for you, you Irish bastard!" whilst telling the rather surprised and agitated public that they encountered to "learn to love the steed or fuck off". But with the flash of a very particular smile, both him and Wesley were off the hook.

Since the incident, Marwood and Wesley had parted ways, and from the incident, Marwood learned something. He learned that Mustangs weren't really his cup of tea and had since bought a bright blue '93 Suzuki Super Carry van, which was large, spacious, and reliable. When a few of his friends commented that it wasn't at all sporty or chic enough, Marwood would first laugh heartily at the term "chic" being applied to him, and then invited them into his van, which quickly shut them up, as he decked it out to appear bigger than most of his friend's living areas. It's not like it was a portal to a different dimension or anything; it was just that Marwood knew how to play Tetris with an almost inhuman level of skill and applied those concepts to the real world. He never told them this, as he feared it would bore them terribly. If he were to explain how he did it though, they would be anything but bored. Marwood, however, was never one to make a fuss about such things. Another thing he wouldn't make a fuss about was the fact that he upgraded aspects of his van with new, and in the case of a certain secret military device dubbed the TeleDrive, never-making-it-to-market technology. Although he tried his best to hide the technological marvel around people, when someone actually did see it, Marwood would take off his glasses, and that person would be none the wiser concerning the custom upgrades to the van, allowing Marwood to temporarily geek out over every aspect (including how he did the Tetrising in the back), without feel guilty about it. He claimed that it was a gift from the gods, but the trouble with Marwood was, he'd be exceptionally vague and wouldn't let slip exactly which god had given it.

--

Rodney stood tall as he exited the bus by his flat.

He wore a rather ordinary dark green coat over his white-buttoned shirt. Ordinarily, he'd wear a navy-blue tie, but he spilled some chicken tikka masala on it at lunch, so despite the fact that the tie itself could have done with more color, it did not align with his company's dress code, even after he cleaned it the best he could.

He sported a rather ordinary middle parted haircut. His hair was dark and straight. When he was younger, he was envious of his curly-haired peers, as they seemed to get all the girls. "The girls love the hair!" His college friend Oliver once said on a night out. Oliver was of Jamaican and African descent and sported quite the afro. "Back in my home country, they say the curly haired men have a zest for life!" Oliver then proceeded to get grinded on by a tall Brazilian woman, whose name no one in that nightclub could pronounce properly.

Rodney led a rather ordinary life. His hair was decidedly, almost by fate, non-curly despite his attempts to correct it otherwise. And he didn't wear his tie out to Indian restaurants outside of work often enough, which was a pity; that tie was a good wingman -- the red, yellow and brown stains fell in just the right way to suit it well in a social atmosphere, and the tie knew it -- what it lacked was the communication skill to drive this point home.

Rodney proceeded down the road. With his laptop bag slung over his shoulder, he began to drift. He was daydreaming of a far better place than this. Bathing in the sun on a white sand beach, drinking margaritas and tequila sunrises whilst reading some esoteric mystery novel that nobody's ever heard of. He had a hard week, and he needed to relax. As he walked along the street towards his flat, he looked up at the clear night sky above him, full of stars. 'Oh, any of those would do...', he idly considered. '...any one of those would do quite nicely for a quick getaway'. But, for now, he had to turn his attention to the present. He had reached his flat door. From his right pocket, he clumsily grabbed his keys. He turned the key in the door and entered.

The flat in which Rodney lived wasn't exactly the cleanest of places. He had old pizza boxes stacked high in a corner next to the kitchen, and dirty clothes strung about all over the place. He had a mattress in his bedroom, but he hardly ever slept on it. He usually ended up sleeping at his desk a mere six feet away, usually on his keyboard, after a night of surfing the web, or when he was in a better state of mind, writing a little poetry.

He sat at the dining table, having navigated through the maze of containers of pizzas past, and poured himself a small glass of scotch. He decided to move to the desk. He fired up the small red laptop which laid upon it and popped open his favorite word processing program. He typed.

Why am I here?

He contemplated this for a few seconds.

For as long as I can remember, I have not been satisfied. Relationships that have been strained, mostly outside of my control. Going from job to job in this economy.

It wasn't just where he lived in England either -- it was a global recession. He sipped his scotch.

Though I am thankful that I can get a job. I know many that cannot, but I digress. I just need a break. I've got to get away.

Suddenly, Rodney felt a small wind of air near his ear. At first, he tried to brush it off, before looking around puzzled. What was that? His mind having scanned the area, Rodney sat back in his chair, and surmised that it must have been a ghost, and he wasn't afraid of ghosts, at least not in the formal manner to which we are all accustomed. When he was five years old, he was in hospital after a biking accident, and had a ghost scare whilst being examined by his doctor. The doctor looked at Rodney with a small smile, leaned in close, put his hand on his little left shoulder and said very softly: "Don't worry about ghosts. No one needs to worry about ghosts. They're too busy bumbling about in their own dimension of existence to bother with us." Rodney, being five years old at the time, didn't really understand what he was talking about, but the way he said it sounded reassuring. The doctor then ruffled his hair and cheerfully announced "You've made a grand recovery, Rodney. Looks like you'll be out of here in a few days!"

Unfortunately, the local news reported that the doctor got knocked down by a double decker bus two weeks later and perished, but as sad as Rodney was to hear about this, whenever he remembered that moment in the hospital, he couldn't help but smile a little. *Right,* he thought, *back to reality...*and his mind slowly sobered up towards the words staring back at him. He realized his writing attempts were going to be fruitless tonight and decided to close the laptop. Upon closing it, he caught sight of his watch. It read a quarter past six. But then he just kept on staring, almost mesmerized by the moving of the hands and the ticking noise they made as they did so.

Dear God, he thought, *it really has been a long week.*

As he looked around at the barren cardboard fortresses around him, Rodney thought back to when he moved into this flat. It was during Marwood's last week in town before going off to be stationed in Afghanistan -- "So let's make it a good one, eh? I want to get so blitzed that tomorrow would feel like reincarnation." In fact, Marwood came up smiling, as he always did after those nights, at 9AM sharp. Rodney, however, felt like he had lived through a thousand lives, only to feel shitty enough to think that he should sleep through another five hundred or so incarnations before tackling the day ahead of him.

This was it! Rodney realized the way out he needed. After all, it had been six years. He went over to the telephone desk in the kitchen (because he didn't cook; he thought he'd put the kitchen to some use). He looked for the little book he kept by his phone, before realizing that before pest control came to get rid of the roaches that infested his apartment due to some leftover pizza he left lying around, he put it in the small drawer just to the left of the stove.

The pizza incident occurred after a particularly unsuccessful date with a therapist a few weeks earlier. On his way home from that, his only thought was to stop at the 24-hour Tesco and pick up lots of beer, get home, and order lots of pizza. He rather successfully made a pity party out of it (complete with Massive Attack's *Mezzanine* album on loop). He didn't emerge from his bedroom for two days, after which his five o'clock shadow had seen quite a few five o'clocks.

He flipped through his little book and found Marwood's number. He picked up his phone with determination. This was his way out. He dialed the number, hoping that the number he had written down still worked.

Marwood was not cursed with the same plight with women that Rodney was. This, however, is not presently of the utmost importance. What is of the utmost importance is this: At the exact moment that Rodney was calling him for the first time in six years, Marwood was doing the dirty between the sheets with some lass he picked up at the department store mere hours earlier. Her name was Lauren, and she was a rather successful criminal lawyer, so she was already a huge fan of Marwood before meeting him. But more than that, she was more curious as to whether there was more to the "wood" in his name, and since he believed in the true freedom of knowledge sharing, he felt the need to oblige her curiosity. When Rodney called, they had been going at it doggy-style on a bed in the back of Marwood's van, and Marwood was rather spank-happy. However, Lauren's curiosity still had not been completely assuaged by the time that the phone went off. Marwood stopped mid-thrust.

"Ignore it!" Lauren demanded. In her line of work, and indeed because of her reputation within it, she was used to getting her way. However, so was Marwood, and his powers of persuasion were greater.

"But I can't. Freedom of knowledge, baby." With that, he exited her, and she sighed, rather disappointingly.

"Sod this, I need a smoke!" Lauren muttered sharply under her breath.

They both put some clothes on hastily. Marwood reached for his phone and pressed "Answer".

"Marwood's Bar and Grill. Owner of the establishment speaking!"

"Marwood... I had no idea you owned a bar..." Rodney started, speaking slowly, and rather deliberately.

Marwood's eyes widened, and he had a flashback to that last night before Afghanistan. Techno remixes of popular 80's and 90's show tunes dominated the DJ decks, as Marwood tried to dominate on the dancefloor, and even managed to convince Rodney to dance with the shy girl in the corner sporting green hair and a tattoo of a white rabbit eating a black dragon on her upper arm.

At this point, Lauren opened the door of the van, bringing Marwood back to reality, and shouted back "Who fucks in the back of a van anyway?!" before exiting and slamming the door as Marwood made some go-away gesture. He then made his way to a small desk on the right-hand side (the back of his van was spacious), reminiscing that, on the whole, he was having a rather great day, causing him to pull a rather cheesy grin.

"Rodney! My main man! Been ages mate. How goes

it?" Nothing was going to rob Marwood of his sunny disposition today, not even an exasperated Englishman. He started playing with a piece of string on the desk, something he regularly did when he was engaged in a secondary activity, such as talking on the phone.

"Not too bad. Just the usual--you know. So, what's with the bar and grill line?"

Marwood dropped the string onto the desk. "It's just a thing to weed out the pranksters." He paused momentarily to collect a thought. "You know mate, I just got some good stuff here recently. The kind that would make you feel like you can see the entirety of time and space and everything. With this, you will be the alpha and the omega...!"

"You know I stopped doing that kind of stuff after Tina left."

"Oh...right. Was just saying is all..." Marwood picked up the string and continued where he left off.

"Right. So, are you free for drinks tonight?" Rodney figured that getting out of the house to go to the pub was about as close to an escape as he was going to get in the short term.

"Uh..." Marwood put down the string again, picked up a nearby copy of War and Peace and flicked through a whole bunch of pages. His ego stopped him from letting people know exactly how much free time he had these days. "...yeah, that works fine. Meet you at The Duchess' Groin?"

"Where is that again?"

"It's just north of The Queen's Legs on Royal Phuck Lane." Marwood said rather straightly, all things considered.

"Ah yes. Been years since I've been there. Let's say 8?"

"Marvelous, see you there Rodders."

"See you."

Rodney put the phone down, which in the case of Rodney meant putting it back on the hook. Despite the constant nagging of everyone who knew him, he still had a landline. He kept on saying he didn't like cell phones because he hated the idea of people always being able to contact him. He liked being sociable as much as the next guy, but when he liked being alone, he did so professionally. He showered, got changed into something a little smarter, and left his flat.

The Duchess' Groin looked like a hole in the wall. The flowery wallpaper indicated no one had decided to change it since the 1970's. Also, except for a few neon signs, it was dark, and thus many people thought Rodney was a bit odd as he entered The Duchess' Groin for one reason: he was wearing sunglasses. He walked in at precisely 8 o'clock, for being unpunctual was a very rude thing to be, in Rodney's mind. He waltzed nonchalantly towards the bar, where he spotted Marwood.

Marwood, on the other hand, had a different philosophy when it came to the timing towards his affairs: he believed in being early for appointments. He thought that if you weren't early, you could miss other opportunities that you might not have had otherwise, such as striking a conversation with the cute girl who works the front desk (although in one particular case with Marwood, it went a bit further than that. He managed to not only get a phone number, but also a few opportunities with her on top of, against, and under the front desk after hours, which definitely made up for the fact that he was there to go through the long and boring process of making sure his insurance claims were in order). However, if you were late, you at least have the opportunity to come up with an interesting backstory as to why (the challenging part, of course, is trying to make it believable -- an acquaintance of Marwood's tried to use the old "my car got eaten by a Velociraptor" trick, which whilst technically true since he crashed into the Natural History Museum and his car went flying into the jaws of a small carnivorous dinosaur, this excuse did not work too well with the people who were interviewing him for a truck driving job). In Marwood's opinion, it was far worse to be on time, because that was what people expected, and Marwood always tried his best to not be what people expected.

Marwood stood as a tall but slightly chubby character dressed in a black suit, which went with his neatly groomed mustache and goatee but contrasted greatly with the white teeth he bore, which a lot of people noticed, as it seemed that he had a permanent grin on his face. The two men made eye contact. Marwood had the kind of eyes that direct contact with them could drag your entire being into his head. Rodney, however, was wearing protective lenses. On the televisions above the bar, there was news footage of the aftermath of some devastation in France. A lot of people who looked at it looked down and shook their heads in despair. An elderly couple at the end of the bar broke down in tears. The world was not the nice place it once was, even a year ago. Everyone knew it, but no one could quite pinpoint what started all of this. Well, except for one man.

"Rodney, you old cunt! Glad you could join!" Marwood exclaimed upon Rodney's approach. They shook hands and patted one another on the back. Behind them, a bartender was pouring enough beers for what seemed like an entire galaxy.

"What's with the sunglasses?" Marwood excitedly inquired.

"Marwood, I have found that I am sensitive to sunlight as of late." Rodney was still dragging his words, but now much less so. A change of atmosphere did wonders for people like Rodney.

"It's pitch black out." Marwood replied.

"Force of habit." Rodney shifted his eyes.

"I see." Marwood raised an eyebrow at Rodney momentarily before suggesting that they move the twelve pints of lager that the bartender had just finished pouring to a nearby table. They found one and sat down.

"Twelve pints? You haven't changed a bit, I see." Rodney remarked, and then he noticed something. He leaned close to Marwood.

"Hang on Marwood, don't you need to pay the bill for that?" Rodney quietly inquired.

Marwood flashed a grin and snorted a quiet laugh. "If you want to find out how, you'd have to take your glasses off first."

Rodney laughed. This was exactly the kind of distraction he needed to escape the mundane nature of something he'd hesitate to call a life.

"But why twelve?" Rodney asked.

"Six for me, six for you. One for each year we have missed each other's company."

"To old times!" Rodney toasted.

"To old times!"

Oddly enough, there were only two notable differences between the old times and the present. The first, and most obvious, was that there was a six-year time difference. Secondly, during old times, and in fact at any point before the present, a man on fire had never run into the bar of The Duchess' Groin screaming a blood curdling scream of death.

Many drunks pointed, made "fire in the hole" jokes and laughed, whilst the more sober amongst them fled for their lives. Rodney and Marwood, however, acting rather like the eye of the storm, stayed at their table, calmly sipping their beers whilst engaged in small conversation.

"Are you still in the Army?" inquired Rodney.

"No. I'm out of it, Rodney. I'm bloody out!" Marwood started tearing up. "It was too much! When Ryan and Tim went over the top, and I saw their bodies later, I just knew--I had to get out of there and come back home."

He looked around and saw the burning corpse near the bar and tried to hold back his tears, but failed to do so, ever so slightly. Rodney sympathetically suggested they go elsewhere. They exited the pub in a somber, but not entirely sober, fashion. Upon exit, Rodney found a piece of paper on the ground crumpled on the ground, a little burned at the edges. He felt a sudden compulsion to examine it further. He picked it up and read.

"Found you. May be a bit obvious by now.
Danger is afoot, but don't worry.
I will find you again."

Still curious, he looked on the other side. It simply said "To Rodney" with some scratching out next to his name that he couldn't quite make out. Though he rationalized that the letter might not have been for him in particular, he made a subconscious decision to keep it, nonetheless.

"Where now?" Marwood asked, putting on his

sunglasses. In the case of an unknown escapade, it's best to be prepared.

Rodney slid the paper in his pocket, mumbling about how this kind of shit could only happen on a Friday night.

"Hmmm, sounds like we need to hit a nightclub..." Marwood suggested.

"Considering all that happened in the last couple of minutes, I'd say a lively atmosphere with interesting drinks would be imperative right now." Rodney replied.

"How about The Devil's Ballroom? I've never actually been there, but I've heard lots of good things." Marwood innocently suggested.

Rodney raised an eyebrow. "Isn't that a gay club?"

"Only on Tuesday nights." Marwood nonchalantly replied. He pushed the ridge of his sunglasses up the bridge of his nose slightly.

"Oh, alright then." Rodney said as he shrugged a little.

They arrived at a castle. The first thing any normal human being would notice about the castle was the purple smoke emitting from the ground surrounding it.

"It's a bit big, isn't it?" Rodney asked.

"Yeah..." Marwood marveled. The castle was indeed very tall, with five fat towers. They approached the doors and noticed a couple of oddities about it: the very large testicle knockers and the *Please Knock!* neon-lit sign at the top. Marwood stroked his beard.

"Well, which one of us is going to lose our dignity now?" Rodney asked. To him, the knockers was the cherry on top of the cake of crazy that his evening had turned into.

"You know Rodney, sometimes you just have to grab life by the balls!" Marwood stopped stroking his beard, rushed slightly towards the door and whacked the left testicle with all his might.

Slowly, the doors opened. Darkness emanated from within. A rough and masculine voice bellowed. *"Welcome to the Ballroom. Admission is free tonight, in light of recent events. Enjoy your stay!"*

Side by side, they entered the abyss.

To the left, there was a security guard whose name plate explained that he was Mike and that he assured public safety. Sitting on a stool, the man was distracted, reading the latest issue of Cosmopolitan. Having caught the pair out of the corner of his eye, he reached out an arm in front of them as if it were a gate.

"IDs please." Mike requested. The men froze, causing him to look up from *"10 Nail Designs to Try This Winter"*.

Marwood took off his glasses and stared at Mike's eyes with what would seem to most to be the hypnotic effect of staring into the depths of infinity. Mike, however, wasn't most. He rolled up his magazine and put it away.

"Look, IDs or you don't get in."

Marwood's grin escaped, off on a quest for a better life. He then put his glasses back on and clumsily reached for his ID. Rodney, being Rodney, gave his ID straight away and apologized profusely for his friend's seemingly strange behavior.

"Oh, we get shit like that all the time." Mike reassured.

"Really?"

"Yeah...and in some cases, people use their actual shit. It's rather disturbing, not to mention a clear violation of most health and safety codes, but more to the point, we can't use that as a valid form of age verification." Mike paused and smirked ever so slightly. "Well, at this club, anyway."

Rodney raised his eyebrows. Then he realized that the night for him was relatively young, and with the way it began, he had better get used to it if he was going to make it through. He went to join his eccentric companion at the bar, who had just ordered five tequila shots.

"Say, barkeep, what would you do if the world was going to end? Would you guys put on some sort of Armageddon disco or something?" Marwood asked.

"Well sort of." The bartender looked Marwood straight in the eyes and grinned, like he was playing poker for the fate of the galaxy, and he had a royal flush. "We'd put on a donkey show in the case that the world ends. We believe in being an ass to our customers if it's the last thing we ever do. Give 'em something to remember us by." The bartender poured the shots. His name was Tony. He had a crew-cut haircut and wonky teeth. He noticed Rodney's approach to the bar, and Marwood noted that Rodney's demeanor had calmed slightly...either he was panicking deep down inside, or he was adjusting to the strangeness of the night. In this case, Marwood was wrong; it was both. Tony laid out the shot glasses upon the bar.

"So, what are we having here, then?" Rodney asked.

"Tequila Surprises, Rodney." Marwood replied.

Rodney noted the odd number of shots Marwood had just ordered.

"Uh, Marwood, why did we order five shots? There's only two of us. I mean assuming we take two shots each--"

"Which we are..." Marwood interrupted sharply.

"Yes, even then, it'd be four. Who's the last shot for?"

Marwood made a gesture to a table on the far-side of the bar.

"The last shot is for Marley's ghost, Rodney." Marwood replied rather coolly. Rodney immediately stared over at the table.

"Has the world of fiction and reality melded together?" He asked. Marwood leaned over and realized Rodney's vantage point was not advantageous; he dragged him over so he could get a completely uninhibited view of the table and its guest.

And it was, indeed, the ghost of Marley. Bob Marley. Smoking a blunt, not having a care in the world. He waved at Rodney, who reluctantly waved back.

"We have one of the best holographic systems in town." Tony started with a big grin. He worked hard to get here, a place where the populace and the amount they tip were parts of an equation that balanced in his favor, so he always took an opportunity to show his pride.

Rodney's eyes started to dart around the room. He then proceeded to patrol the edges of the room, and even, with Mike's permission, exited the building, and stared at the roof. No signs of any boxes -- anything that could be used for magnetic or projection purposes, or indeed any sort of extra equipment aside from the roof itself. With the items on his vague mental checklist remaining unchecked, he quickly went back inside and rejoined Marwood at the bar.

"Wow, that must be one of the best...there's no visible apparatus." Rodney stated to Tony. Tony gave Rodney a nod of satisfaction.

At this point, Marwood's features scrunched up, as if he just saw a car wreck, and then his face dropped, like he suddenly became preoccupied. He immediately slammed through his two shots and urged Rodney to do the same, which he did rather reluctantly. He put his arm around

Rodney's shoulder.

"Rod---" Marwood started, interrupted by a slight burp and a burning in his chest. "Rodney, I must talk with you outside. There are matters..." His speech slurred ever so slightly. "...that we must discuss." He turned them towards the door. They started stumbling towards it.

"Is there anything more you need?" Tony asked.

Marwood let out a large belch, which was just what he needed. He then turned towards Tony with a big grin and two thumbs up. "Just make sure old Bob there gets his shot." He paused to compose himself a little. "And if I were you, I'd start looking for that donkey now!"

As they were going towards the door, Mike, sitting back in his chair, blocked them with his legs. He looked up from his magazine. Upon making eye contact with Marwood, he threw the magazine behind him, snapped his fingers, and rose to his feet.

"You." He said to Marwood intensely.

"Me." Marwood replied with a smirk. At this point, he looked Mike up and down, and thought "*Yes, if the opportunity for mud wrestling came up, I could definitely take on this security guard.*"

"You worked it out." Mike mentioned.

"Wasn't hard." Marwood snickered.

Rodney looked at Mike. Then back at Marwood. Then back at Mike.

"Wait a second..." Rodney started. Marwood went all bug-eyed. Rodney shouldn't know about this. At all. No. Not his business, surely.

"Earlier, I felt a ghost by my desk..."

At this point, Marwood rolled his eyes. "We don't have time for this..."

Suddenly, the lights went down, and a spotlight

shone on the two men.

"Time, gentlemen. Time is a funny thing." Mike replied. "Do not be concerned with time..." He bore a mischievous grin. "...for once you leave tonight, you will have no memory of what took place here tonight. So, in essence, you have all the time in the world." With that, he snapped his fingers.

The next thing Rodney remembered was the phone. The phone was ringing. As was his head.

'Dammit' was his first thought. His second thought was 'Should have unplugged the bastard when I left last night.' Well, he was now awake, so he might as well answer it. Oh, so much pain. "...the fuck did I drink last night?" he murmured to himself, as he picked up the phone.

"Rodney!!! I'm having such a smashing time up here!" It was his sister, Caroline. He groaned inside his head. He had a hangover the size of Jupiter, and the last thing he needed was highly enthusiastic and very annoying, not to mention boring and just plain tedious, discourse from his holiday-making sister. She was on an all-inclusive trip in Florida with the family. Her husband, Bill, came from a rich family, so they could afford to do things like that on a whim. "The kids had a fabulous time in Disney World, and I'm loving the sun here! Free drinks too! We went to play tennis the other day, and Bill was kicking everyone's arse! The hotel is putting on a tournament tomorrow morning and I'm sure he'll win!"

"That's great Caroline..." He really couldn't get a word in edgeways here, as the woman clearly didn't know when to shut the hell up.

"...and Oh My God! Charlie got a little Mickey costume,

and he looks so cute! You should have seen him! I got pics! I'll show you lots of pics when I get back!"

"Caroline. It's 4 in the goddamned morning. I have work tomorrow." His brain pounded on the walls of his skull demanding a decent go at sleep.

"4 in the morning? Oh...yeah...I guess we did have to change our watches when we were on the plane. Oh well, I went to the massage parlor yesterday and Oh My God that felt so good! It was free too! They really could make a killing if they charged for these things." Rodney was about to point out the obvious here, but he figured it just wasn't worth the effort.

"Anyway Caroline...I have to go... I'm glad you're having a fun time and I'm sure I'll see you soon after you get back."

"Goodness, is everything alright Rodney?!"

He sighed. "Yes, everything's fine. I just need to get some more shut eye." His brain breathed a sigh of relief, knowing rest would be coming soon.

"Well, ok then. Sweet dreams!" She then started singing "So long! Farewell! Auf Wiedersehen! Goodbye!" They hung up. She always said goodbye that way, and it annoyed the crap out of him every time. She only took a liking to those kinds of songs once the kids came along, and Rodney had a feeling that this kind of thing wasn't going to end anytime soon. He collapsed onto his mattress for the second time that week.

Rodney heard his front door open, and footsteps, rather daintily, making their way into the living room. At this point, Rodney jumped out of his bed to see what was going on. There was a naked woman in his flat. Rodney was puzzled as to why she was there. Especially since he didn't know her. He did, however, estimate she was in her mid-20s and noted that her hair was a shade of color that his brain had not previously registered.

"Do not be alarmed." She said, followed by a small flirtatious giggle.

Rodney was still speechless. Random girl in the flat was one thing. Random naked girl was quite another game. One that involved quite a few dice.

"That note earlier was meant for your eyes, and your eyes alone."

'Oh good' He thought, before immediately becoming more puzzled as to why she was there.

"Wh...Wh...Wh..." was the best he could muster at this time.

"Shhhh…" She started. "Right now, it doesn't matter." Her deep mud-brown-eyes connected with his. "I want you."

She walked over to him.

"I want you to take me and do with me as you will," she said with a voice as smooth as silk and as soft as a white rabbit. Her hands caressed his arms, pulling herself slowly towards him. She tilted her head towards his and they kissed. She stuffed a scrunched-up piece of paper with random numbers into his hand, of which he caught a momentary glimpse.

And then there was the crack of thunder.

Rodney suddenly awoke to a storm worthy of existing only in the great plains of North America on a late spring afternoon. He tried to compose himself, whilst also dealing with the disappointment that the most recent event had only been a dream.

This disappointment lingered around in an annoying way for a few minutes. It was brushed away by a feeling of confusion, when next to his mattress, he found a scrunched-up piece of paper with the very same random numbers he had seen previously. He looked at his digital clock radio. It bore the reading 7:30 which shone like a steady beacon of light against the highly playful and unstable light situation that he could clearly see from his bedroom window. He briefly wondered if this was a metaphor for his love life but figured that the chances of finding someone quite as stable as the light from his clock radio would be a fine thing. Then the power cut out, causing the light from the clock radio to blink out of existence, and Rodney determined that this was definitely the aforementioned metaphor. He sighed, and figured that with the power out, it would be the best time for him to get some more sleep.

When Rodney woke up, the power had been restored. He sat at the dining table, looked at the piece of paper, and contemplated. He contemplated how the one who gave him the paper was probably no different from the other girls he had been with, as evidenced by the fact that she wouldn't tell him what the devil was going on. Images of the succubae from his past crowded his mind. They started marching--marching to the Imperial March from Star Wars. That could only mean one thing. Someone was at the door, and Rodney muttered to himself, "I really do need to change that bloody doorbell".

Speaking of the devil, and this is the last it shall be spoken of for quite some time, it was Marwood at the door. He was wearing the same pair of sunglasses from the previous night, and as always, bearing that huge charismatic grin. He was also carrying a laptop bag.

"Just came back to check on you, Rodders--you were pretty gone last night after we had that Tequila Surprise."

It should be evident at this point that not only did Mike underestimate Rodney's companion, but given that he actually remembered the night, he was in what one would consider an impossibly chipper mood for 9 o'clock the very next morning.

"Thanks, Marwood...you know, I forgot...what was in that Tequila Surprise?" Rodney's tiredness was still getting the better of him.

"Eh...grenadine, lime juice..."

"...and obviously tequila?"

"...actually, no. That was the surprise part. It was Everclear." His grin parted ways with him in a very understandable fashion. They had an arrangement. It would soon be back.

"Jeez, no wonder my brain feels backed up--"

"You mean like a highway sandwich?"

"...eh?"

"Your brain. Feels like two completely separated parts sandwiched together and smeared with traffic jam." Marwood's grin came running back for a fleeting moment. Rodney scratched his head a bit.

"Uh...yeah. Anyway, I have something I want you to take a look at."

They walked over to the dining table. Rodney presented Marwood with the piece of paper. Marwood stared at the paper, and as he figured that further investigation was imperative, a slow smile crept across his face. Marwood got out his laptop and a magnifying glass. In the case that serious detective work would be needed, Marwood wanted to show the world that he meant business.

The piece of paper read as follows: *52 58 1 10*

"Lottery numbers, you think?" Inquired Rodney,

observing Marwood giving the paper a once over with the magnifying glass.

"Nah, can't be. Not enough numbers, and anyway...the lottery only goes up to fifty-six. This is something different. Something not entirely...random. Four numbers...shaping a whole. A group...with each number being a piece of the puzzle, a piece of the pie. A pie divided into four pieces, but much more practical. Rodney, can you think of anything?"

Rodney contemplated this for a second, and then decided he could do with a snack to think on. He went to the fruit bowl and got two apples.

"Apple?" offered Rodney.

"Apple? Brilliant!" Marwood took the apple and started typing on his laptop.

"What? How?"

"Apples...they each have a core...just like the Earth. Four numbers and the Earth..."

Marwood snapped his fingers. "...must be latitude and longitude!"

"Really? How in the fuck did you get that?"

Marwood grinned. "What else could it possibly be?"

"Anything. Hell, it could be part of someone's phone number."

"How did it come to you again?"

"It was in a dream."

"Ah. Well, if you believe in fate..." Marwood started preaching. Rodney knew where this was going, and he didn't have the patience to go through six hours of it, so he stopped it in its tracks.

"Okay, okay. So. Assuming it is latitude and longitude, for all we know, it could take us to Mexico or Zimbabwe or something."

"Actually, I just typed the coordinates into the laptop, and it gives us...Nottingham." Marwood's mind was clicking away at some basic calculations. "That's only a few hours away. Even if it isn't the case, it's not like we'd lose much."

Rodney knew his friend well and ran the same calculations though his head. "Just a bit of time--not too bad, I suppose."

"You ready then?" Marwood sensed that time was of the essence.

"What? I have to work today..."

"No, you don't--it's Saturday, you muppet." Marwood pulled a stupid, but highly amusing facial expression.

Because of what had occurred earlier, Rodney's relationship with time was on the rocks. He suspected it was cheating on him with someone who had a better tie collection. "Oh, yeah. Alright then." Rodney packed a bag of essentials and said goodbye to the flat.

They took Marwood's van and embarked on the three-hour journey north.

CHAPTER 2

STORMY BEGINNINGS PART 2

For the entirety of human history, man always wondered about the concept of a creator--a higher being. There has been much commotion over this, as not only could men never really agree on which higher being it was that created the Earth, but they couldn't even agree on the number of higher beings involved with the Earth. In truth, though, there was just one higher being that was involved with the Earth. His name was Ben--and he really couldn't understand why this whole business was the cause of most of the wars on the planet. This, as far as he could remember, was never part of the contract he signed. The contract, however, did state "a casual work environment," and Ben definitely took stock in that. He was an avid musician and even moved a piano into his office, which was the size of an entire galaxy (after all, they promised roomy work environments). An interesting side effect of playing the piano, though, whilst he was on the job, was that it would cause various weather effects to occur over the part of the planet he happened to be watching over at the time. He was presently playing Greensleeves, watching over the part of the M1 motorway connecting London to the Midlands-- causing a light drizzle over the area.

Up ahead was a storm brewing--a storm that neither Ben with his music, nor nature itself could have caused. He stared at the thing, rather puzzled, and phoned his supervisor.

--

The M1 was crowded. It was jam-packed full of day-trippers, Saturday shoppers, weekend businesspeople and regular trippers who had a serious case of the munchies. Marwood and Rodney remained calm through all this though, after all they had all the time in the world. Or so they thought.

The storm started off innocently enough, as most thunderstorms do. It quickly lost its virginity however by artificial means and ballooned to be about the size of the entirety of middle England, which curiously enough, was the area it was moving towards.

The front of Marwood's van was, essentially, in a state of constant disarray. He always claimed that it helped him go; that the mess was a source of inspiration, but both him and Rodney knew that he was just lazy. The odd Burger King drink cup here, the odd philosophy book there (which oddly enough, he used to stash his marijuana. He claimed that the type he carried was so sacred, a philosophy book was the best place to store it), and an empty packet of Skittles actually taped to the dashboard, which Marwood claimed he needed, in case he ever came across a hitchhiking leprechaun, believing that the Irish fairy would somehow become one with the rainbow on the packet and magically lead him to the nearest pot of gold.

Crawling up the M1 was a tall and skinny Black man in rags. He wasn't literally crawling of course -- he had enough years on him to suggest that he had made it to the walking stage of life, but he was moving at the pace of a crawl. His expression flittered between blind fury and deep but disconnected euphoria, which seemed to further fuel the fury. When the anger hit, he would hit the nearest car door, and when the person inside the car wound down the window to tell him to fuck off, he would lower his eyelids, bare a shit-eating grin, and tell of how wonderful the world was. Jehovah's witnesses could learn a thing or two from this man. When he got to Marwood's van though, things were different; the euphoria completely lost its signal, and he knew instinctively that the nearest tower was far, far, away.

Bang, bang. Rodney unwound his window, looking rather bewildered.

"You got Charlie here?!" the man bellowed.

"There's no one by that name here, sorry." replied Rodney.

"You're lying."

"No, I can assure you, we are not."

"You lying bastard!" The man pulled out a .38 Special and aimed it straight at Rodney's face, which at this point was as white as a sheet. Rodney, being Rodney, almost shat himself. "You get me Charlie right now or I'll blow yer fuckin' thinking box right out the back o'your skull, alright?!"

"Bu-bu-bu-" was all Rodney could muster in his theoretically brown stained trousers.

Marwood put his hand on Rodney's shoulder and leaned over.

"Look, mate, we ain't got no Charlie here right now." Marwood took off his sunglasses and stared at the man eye to eye, with a huge grin across his face. "However, if you get in the van, and help us on our escapade, we can make it worth your while. "

The man, hypnotized, put the gun away.

"Now--get in the back of the van." Marwood said calmly. The man got in the van, and Marwood put his sunglasses back on.

"Marwood, are you sure we can trust him?" Rodney whispered sharply.

Marwood looked back at the man and the man gave Marwood a remorseful frown. The man eyed a copy of Martin Heidegger's "Being and Time" lying near the central console. He smiled, knowing what it meant, and began to relax slightly. Marwood shrugged. "I s'pose."

"A bit dim-witted of you to let him climb aboard don't you think?"

"Look, we don't know what's waiting for us at our destination. For all you know, it could be an ambush by a group of hungry cannibals, and if it is, you're really going to be wishing we had a man armed with a gun when sharp teeth start ripping through our tender flesh."

Rodney hated the way Marwood would put things in his more universal perspective sometimes. Silence crept into the van, made itself comfy, and stayed for a while.

The storm itself looked like no storm anyone could have ever seen before. It had some lightning and wind, which of course many would say was perfectly natural. What wasn't perfectly natural, however, was the dark blue and dark green vortex that seemed to engulf the entire area. Even stranger was the fact that it didn't appear to be doing anything as nothing appeared to be sucked into it. It just went on for miles, whirling in the normal way vortexes do with the occasional strike of lightning and gusts of wind, and then disappearing somewhere around Leeds (though some say that's always where the true weirdness begins). This was the kind of thing that made weather forecasters throw their hands up in the air, hand in their notice and start a new occupation of hiding under the coffee table in their living room, suffering from panic attacks. In fact, that was exactly what many weather forecasters in the area did that day.

Ben's supervisor, Jeff, came into Ben's office to see what the problem was. Ben pointed at the storm. Jeff looked shocked.

"They...have...returned..." Jeff whispered slowly. "...I never thought they would."

--

Somewhere around the center of the storm, a motorcyclist just got pulled over by two cops, one tall and fat, the other short and skinny. Having tended to a number of supernatural incidents recently, it would be considered a miracle that these cops were still alive. But with all this, there is still a price; before any of this happened, the fat one was skinny and the skinny one was fat. Together, they had seen shit that would make Cthulhu squint in disgust. So, pulling over a motorcyclist speeding at a level that seemed to them to be otherworldly, was just another thing to mark off the bucket list at this point.

"What seems to be the problem, officers?" asked the motorcyclist.

"Please remove your helmet sir." requested the fat one.

"Well, I'd rather not, if it's all the same to you, Dunkin Donuts."

The small one nudged the fat one as if to say "just get on it with it so we can get some lunch around here".

"Sir, you were doing 410 in a 70 zone--" The cop

sighed. There was no protocol for this, and he knew what the risks were. "We're going to have to write you a ticket for that. Can I see proof of insurance and a valid ID?"

"I really do have otherworldly matters to attend to. If I were you, I'd just let this one go, fellas."

The cops briefly smirked at each other and turned back. "Sir, we are here to uphold the law. Insurance and license, please."

"You'll regret it. . .but if you really want it, sure thing, it's somewhere between shove it up your arse and burn in Hell."

"Excuse me sir?!"

"Well, the last part at least." He pointed at the fat man, and the man became engulfed in flames. With the man screaming, the helmeted one snapped his fingers, and the vortex was now whirling faster and sucking in small debris off the road.

The motorcyclist turned to the short man, and asked calmly and quietly: "You want my ID?"

The short man whimpered. The motorcyclist removed his helmet to reveal a man with long blonde hair.

"My name is Christian Lucifer--Leader of the Associate Guardians of the Underworld." Several men dressed in black suits walked up to him out of the darkness. "Something has gone very wrong, and we are terribly pissed off." With that, he snapped his fingers again, sending the short man flying into the vortex. A middle-aged woman, being rather pissed off with the fact that a group of strange men were standing around in the middle of a motorway, honked at and then drove around them, screaming bad things about Christian's mother. If she knew Christian's mother though, she would want to take back all the things she had just said--whether she had the chance to or not was another matter, and she would have to be extremely lucky to even get that chance.

Rodney turned to his guest in the back of the van.

"So, what's your name?"

"Nigel. Nigel Locosa."

"And what is your deal, Nigel?"

"Well, I can get you a good price for some very upmarket LSD..."

Rodney rolled his eyes. "I mean, what is your deal? Why are you begging at the side of a motorway?"

"I... I used to be a salesman in a software shop, but that was before the recession hit. That's when I decided to sell drugs full-time. Was making some pretty good money there for a while too, but then people stopped buying, and I was left to beg on the streets, looking for what drugs I could find...even using violence to get my way."

Rodney's expression dropped. "Sad story, that..." He paused and made a gun symbol with his hand. "...so, how many people have you killed using that thing?"

"None yet...they always tend to give me the stuff. Quite lucky actually. Must be all these trippers on the road. But it will be two if you lot don't get me any after we're done with...whatever the fuck we're doing. What the fuck are we doing anyway?!"

"As weird as it sounds, we're going to a place that has these coordinates." Rodney handed Nigel the paper.

"That is weird." He examined the paper further. And then his mind drifted slightly...to the last weird encounter he had. "You know what else was weird? My last sale. It happened a couple of days ago, it was this guy with long black hair, dressed in motorbike gear."

"What's so interesting about that?"

"Well, he just pointed at my hand and money just appeared. He also said that the hash would be good for all the guys down there, something about how they needed to chill the fuck out. I meant to ask him more questions. Which is weird, because in this business…" He paused for breath and let his brain synchronize with his mouth. He sighed. "In this business, you have to be discreet. Don't ask questions if you don't have to. But this dude…I could tell he was different. That he was someone…"

"Out of this world?" Marwood playfully suggested.

Nigel paused in thought "…yeah." Marwood raised his eyebrows.

"So, what did he say?" Rodney asked.

"Nothing. Didn't get a chance to say shit. Before I knew it, he pointed downwards and disappeared. Really made me wonder what the fuck I was on that day."

Marwood slammed on the brakes and stopped the van.

"Wait, repeat that again?" He inquired.

"What, the disappearing?" asked Nigel.

"Yeah. I mean, how?"

"He pointed downwards, a ring of light appeared around him and he just…disappeared. Why is this important?"

Marwood took a deep breath. "More than you can possibly imagine."

"How?"

"There are forces that are unknown to most around here at work."

"…and just what the fuck does that mean?" Nigel put his hand on his gun just in case he needed it.

"It means, my good sir." Marwood turned slightly, got Nigel in his peripheral vision, and let out a sizable sigh. "That once you take your hand off that please, Mr. Locosa--"

Nigel took his hand off his gun. "Thank you." Marwood whispered. "...we can embark on our escapade."

"Excuse me, but would somebody tell me what the hell is going on? Neither of you are making any sense whatsoever, and we're apparently heading into a massive storm with swirly things." Nigel remarked.

"Storm with sw...oh fuck. Hang on, kids." Marwood instructed.

"Why?" inquired Rodney.

Marwood paused. "You know I've always liked to tinker with things? Well, I grabbed a TeleDrive from the Army research lab, and hooked up an interface for it, so in case of emergency we can just teleport to our destination."

"Which is Nottingham, right?"

"Um, no."

"What do you mean no? It's what the paper said."

"Yeah, well, bollocks to the paper."

"But this really pretty, naked woman gave it to me. . ."

Nigel's ears perked up "You had a hot horny naked bitch direct you to this place?! I say let's go! Who knows what kind of crazy-ass kinky action we can get up there with the hunnies..."

"Nigel, stay out of this." directed Marwood "We're not going to Nottingham. We can't go back there. At least not for a while. I'm sorry, we just can't."

"Why?" Both men asked.

"I'll explain later. Look..." Marwood sighed "...Look, I'll just have to explain later. First, we need to get out of here.

Rodney, could you just pull on the lever inside the glove compartment, please?"

Rodney opened the glove compartment and pulled the bright green lever that seemed to radiate some weird green energy. Marwood pushed the horn on the steering wheel. The van started shaking violently and then faded from the motorway. The people in the vehicles surrounding them at the time would have been weirded out by all this, but these were the same people with a serious case of the munchies.

"Wh-Wh-Wh-Where are we g-g-going?" inquired Rodney. All they could see was black, and the van was still shaking.

"Fr-Fr-Fr-France. They'll never find us th-th-th-there." Marwood replied, as he read the reading on the device. The shaking then stopped, and there was a feeling that the van was moving smoothly. They also had the illusion that they were flying up in the sky. They technically weren't, but the TeleDrive had a process in it which grabbed some environmental data from the destination and surrounded the ship with an interpretation of this data, in order to put the passengers at ease during their travel. It was an older model they were using--newer models could teleport to their destinations a lot quicker and made some very cool "woosh, woosh" noises. The passengers in this case felt anything but at ease. Rodney thought he was going to get sick. Nigel seemed very confused and kept on looking around him like a rabbit in the middle of a busy road trying to figure out its best way to safety. And Marwood just grinned. After a while, the van stopped moving completely, allowing everyone to settle back down slightly.

"Why would they not find us in France?" Rodney

asked.

"Because it's fucking France, Rodney." Marwood paused. He wiped a small bit of sweat from his brow. "Look, I said I'll explain later, and I will."

"Ok, Marwood." Rodney said reluctantly. He figured now was not the time to argue. "You are designated driver after all."

Nigel's ears perked again "Designated driver? Does that mean we can go to a pub, get absolutely smashed, and maybe bang a few chicks?"

Marwood and Rodney turned to Nigel and simultaneously exclaimed "NO!"

Air started bustling around and an old battered but very hi-tech looking '93 Suzuki van appeared in what seemed to be the middle of nowhere, but because of a communications feature that was enabled in the TeleDrive, the middle of nowhere was actually expecting this to happen, but it noted that this was a little out of the ordinary.

CHAPTER 3
THE GAYEST TIME OF THEIR LIVES

It wasn't until the landing that everyone managed to actually collect their thoughts and catch their breath.

Wide-eyed, Rodney stared at the glove compartment, which had just snapped itself shut. A little shaken up, he asked what any polite, well-meaning English gentlemen would ask: "How *the fuck* did we do that?!"

"What do you mean?" asked Marwood.

"The TeleDrive. I mean how the...? what the...?" Rodney was at a loss for words.

Marwood put his hand on Rodney's shoulder.

"Look, I was involved with a special department at the Army developing some high-grade technology. Remember when I said I got out because of the war casualties?"

"Yeah?"

Marwood's face dropped slightly. "I was lying."

"Oh."

Marwood perked up a bit. "Well, only partially. It's a good politically correct excuse; those deaths did affect me quite a bit, don't get me wrong--and I could never go back there, but that's not the reason."

Rodney thought intently for a second. "...is it because you stole their secret research, violated a non-disclosure agreement, and made a TeleDrive of your own?"

"No, fuck that shit. I may be brilliant, but I don't have the fucking time to develop a teleportation device, even with the blueprints!" Marwood dropped his tone as if he were about to confess the wrongdoings of the entire universe. "I just went in there after hours and stole the damned thing."

"Is that why we couldn't go to Nottingham? Because they could catch you there?"

"No, it's not..."

"Then why can't we go to Nottingham?" Rodney asked.

"I'll explain later. Right now, I need a fucking pint-- this teleportation nonsense has made me really thirsty. Let's find a pub." With that, all three men left the van. Marwood didn't know exactly why they had to abandon their mission to Nottingham, but he had seen those kinds of storms before, and knew that it was not something any of them were prepared for at that point in time.

They walked around, trying desperately to find a way out, to find civilization. There was an eerie feeling about the place, and Rodney was convinced they were going around in circles.

"What the hell happened here?" asked Rodney, in an attempt to turn at least something in a productive direction.

"Remember the pub last night?" Marwood asked.

"...barely!" Rodney replied with a slight laugh. Then, with a single thought, his expression dropped. He remembered the atmosphere of the pub when he entered. So solemn, so dreary. But with it being England, he never gave it a second thought. Also, with him being English, he was a bit too wrapped up in his own issues to really be aware of the world around him. Marwood on the other hand, was not your typical Englishman, and was only too aware of the recent events.

"Remember on the news a few months ago, there was an invasion in certain parts of France..." started Marwood.

Rodney was searching his consciousness for any semblance of a memory. "Vaguely. You know it was weird because from what I remember it was headlining one day, and then barely anything was said. Three days later, I don't remember it being on the news at all, and it's not like they don't usually cover these things. Even stranger was the fact that the invaders were never revealed."

"...that was a hush-up. It was a full-on invasion; the country didn't stand a chance, and western civilization isn't accustomed to the basic death of a fellow nation like this, so they just hushed it up, and anyone who asked was denied a true answer. Indeed no one who knew who the invaders were could report anything--anyone who even saw anything ended up dead." Marwood revealed.

"Then why are we here?"

"It was where the van dropped us off."

"You mean the TeleDrive?"

"The TeleDrive engaged the van, yes. When you pulled that green lever, it enacted the emergency procedure--"

"Emergency procedure?"

"Get us the fuck out of where we are. Take us to the nearest safest place."

"Which is a random French slum."

Marwood sighed. "...apparently." He knew the place wasn't always a slum.

Nigel perked up. "...and anyway, how do you know all

this anyway?"

"I have my sources, but I thought it was just a rumor--folklore if you will. I guess it was all true."

"Well, I guess we better get back to the van before we get killed, eh?"

"Nah, I think we're safe from them now. The same sources said they left just as quickly as they came." Marwood scratched the back of his head thoughtfully, walked up to Nigel and put his hand on his shoulder. "...and anyway, Nige," Marwood flashed a grin "...trust the TeleDrive. It cannot steer us wrong." He patted Nigel on the shoulder, and then wandered off.

After wandering through the streets for a while, Rodney's ears perked up, hearing some distant chatter and the sound of clinking glasses. "Hey guys, I think I found that pub we were looking for." Both men ran towards Rodney and looked in the direction he was pointing.

"That's a fucking shack." Nigel noted.

"Yes, but it's a populated shack. They're usually the best anyway. I say let's go." Rodney suggested.

All the men agreed that it was a good idea. The only thing that it said on the shack was the name "Slosh House o' the West" with the labels "We speak English" and "Drink til the Cows come home!" They entered.

As the men entered, they could not help but notice that the saloon was full of cowboys (and indeed, cowgirls). In the corner, they could see a jukebox blaring out country music. It looked like a normal Western Saloon bar, except everyone was actually getting along, and there wasn't so much as a murmur of disagreement among them. The only victim of physical or verbal abuse, to any degree, was in fact, the jukebox. It wasn't the jukebox's fault of course, that on occasion the music would jump or loop, much to the frustration of the patrons. Poor jukebox.

"What part of this is French?!" Nigel exclaimed upon entering.

"I don't know, but I'm sure there is a reasonable explanation for all this." said Rodney, who, by now, was surprised by very little. They walked up to the bar.

"What'll it be guys?" asked the bartender, who bore an American accent.

"A pint of Boddington's, and whatever the others are having." Marwood requested. The others agreed amongst themselves that after all the shit they'd been through, a tequila shot would be the best way to take the edge off.

"...and two tequila shots." Rodney replied.

"What kind of tequila, sir?"

"Whatever you have as the house tequila will be good enough for now..." Rodney felt his words trailing away from him slightly at this point.

"Very good choice, sir." The bartender said with a hint of a smirk. "They will be out soon."

The men scoped out the surprisingly large space. As Rodney's and Nigel's eyes widened, Marwood looked deep in thought. He was fumbling with something in his pocket, but decided that, given that his companions were overwhelmed, his audience questionable, and the object quite a spectacle, now was not the time for a reveal.

"I once heard of a race of people who lived in saloon bars..." Marwood explained. "...but they lost a drinking bet, and consequently their planet was destroyed."

Nigel chimed in. "Wait a second...that bartender...he's not French." However, this remark fell upon deaf ears.

Rodney and Nigel noticed the bar had twenty-four

pool tables, twelve shuffleboard tables (which were all scattered randomly throughout the pub), and eight dart boards on the far wall. Nigel and Rodney were beside themselves. "How could a pub, looking that small from the outside, contain such a volume of space on the inside?", both thought. This thought, however, was very brief, because at that point, the drinks came.

"Right, what shall we toast to?" Nigel asked.

"Marmite?" Marwood suggested.

"Toast to, Marwood--not what you want on your toast, you pillock." Rodney remarked.

"Oh. Hmmm. Vive la France!"

"Vive la France!" They all tapped glasses, carefully, to not spill the shots, and drank. Nigel and Rodney slammed their glasses on the bar and walked towards one of the more randomly placed pool tables.

"Fancy a game?" Nigel inquired.

"Oh, I can kick your homeless arse at pool anytime!" challenged Rodney.

They approached the table. Nigel got all the balls from the holder in the cabinet side and racked them up, whilst Rodney went to get the cues. Once this was complete, Rodney fished around in his pocket and after a few seconds, his hand emerged with a penny.

"Heads, please Rodney." Nigel requested. Rodney nodded. He tossed the coin. It came up tails. And thus, the game of pool between them began.

Marwood, still sitting at the bar, ordered another round of tequila shots (this time with himself included), and noticed a shadowy figure at the other end of the bar. The man was dressed in a leather jacket and sipping a glass of, as far as Marwood could tell, 18-year single malt scotch. One would assume that because of this, that meant the man had money, however those assumptions would be incorrect -- the man had no need for money. The how's and why's surrounding this will later be revealed, but it must be emphasized that this is but a trivial matter. The man, upon finishing his drink, lifted the glass and examined it, as if he could see the sand from which the glass was made. Indeed, if one knew this man well enough, one would actually expect this to be the case. It is at this moment that he caught the glance of Marwood and immediately slammed the glass down on the bar. The man locked eyes with Marwood and moved closer to him.

"Hello Marwood." The man started. "You may not know me -- my name is not important right now, but I do know why you are here."

Marwood raised his eyebrows. "Wait a second. How do you know my name?" He squinted at the man...turned his head to the side, going through his mental rolodex of faces, face shapes and eyes. He noticed a momentary diamond-shaped sparkle in the man's right eye, but in his experience, that didn't mean a whole lot. He got an alien vibe for sure, but he got that very same vibe from Welsh people. With his elbow propped upon the bar, and his hand resting upon his chin, he thought for a few more seconds.

"Where are you from?" Marwood asked.

The man laughed briefly. "Oh, of all the questions, that has to be the least important."

Marwood didn't miss a beat. "So why do you think I'm here?"

"I think you are here because you are trying to escape."

Marwood shifted his eyes. "Yeah, so?"

"You cannot escape for long my friend, and those that come for you -- they need you."

"How do you know that?"

"Because I have seen everything that has happened and what is to be."

"Is that so?" Marwood asked. He took his arms off the bar and folded them. "Stop fucking around and get to the point."

"Look at this bar, Marwood. A Western saloon in La Courneuve, France?! Which has been reduced to a slum?! Come on..."

"It's a trap?"

"I almost wish that was the case, for everyone's sake." He gave a wink.

"Just who the hell are you?!" Marwood demanded.

"I exist within the shadows...of the space-time continuum."

"Isn't that a bit cliché in this day and age?"

"Can you do this?" The man disappeared and reappeared behind Marwood.

"No, I guess not. Even my TeleDrive can't do it that quickly; that must be really high-grade technology. How the hell do you do that?!"

The mysterious one laughed in a semi-empathetic manner. Marwood noticed that except for his companions, his partner in conversation and the bartender that was serving them drinks, the other patrons stopped moving; the place seemed suddenly a bit dead. Rodney and Nigel stopped their game and looked around.

"What the fuck?!" Nigel exclaimed.

"I really don't know..." Rodney replied.

Back at the bar, Marwood was starting to get very fidgety, very fast. The man shifted back in his seat. Marwood held his head in his hands a couple of times, before words could come to him.

"What did you *do?!*" Marwood boomed.

"What?"

Marwood pointed to the rest of the bar. "What did you do to the rest of the patrons here!"

"I did nothing." The shadowy figure answered. "Remember what I mentioned before; a western bar in the middle of a French slum, which by the way is completely deserted otherwise." At this point, Rodney and Nigel figured they'd be here for a while with this fiasco going on and continued their game.

"...and what the fuck is that supposed to mean, Mister Fancy Pants?!" Marwood was getting impatient.

"It means..." The man placed his hand upon Marwood's shoulder. "...look, calm down." Marwood shoved the man's hand off his shoulder. The man raised both arms up in the air, before leaning towards him.

"Marwood. Look, you're better than this. You know for a fact this wasn't my doing--" His eye sparkled again.

"--so, you're just in the wrong place at the wrong time?"

"Well, I wouldn't say that. At least we met."

Marwood groaned. He hated how strangers could be so cheesy sometimes.

The man looked down at his watch.

Each of the twelve faces glimmered a bright blue, whilst the hands themselves shone green. Every face was carved from various kinds of highly rare stones from twelve different planets spanning six systems in a galaxy so far away that many would consider it the opposite end of the universe. The hands were carved by a merchant on a planet in a completely different galaxy. The raw materials for which were bought at a local auction for the Earth American equivalent of $1.99 each. The man's father put it all together just in time for the man's seventeenth birthday. The man briefly smiled remembering the occasion, before turning his attention back to Marwood.

"Look, I gotta go. Why don't you join your friends over there for a game of Cut-Throat?" The man suggested.

Marwood took a deep breath and sighed. "Sounds a bit violent, doesn't it?"

The man gave a hearty laugh. Marwood flashed a small smile.

Then the man disappeared--without paying his tab. Marwood shrugged, and if he didn't know any better, he would think that too many people were stealing technology that was the exclusive property of the British Army. He amused himself with the fact that if the mysterious man ever got caught, he could never get prosecuted because he could just choose to simply not exist in that time period.

Nigel was the last to score a ball in a pocket. Marwood walked over and noticed that the two and ten balls had yet to be pocketed, in addition to the 8 ball.

"Haha, it looks like you both have to get rid of your blue balls before you can think of winning." joked Marwood.

Nigel and Rodney sighed, then continued with their game. They ordered another round of drinks.

The bartender approached the men with a tray containing their drinks. He put them on a nearby table, and approached the men, as if there was a matter of grave importance he meant to bring up. Before he could speak a word, he was cut off.

"What is it with this place?" Marwood asked.

"What about it?" The bartender retorted.

"I mean, present company excluded..." Marwood paused for breath. His previous encounter took a bit out of him. "...this place is completely deserted."

The bartender smiled. "Which makes me even more pleased to serve you guys."

"No, I mean, seriously --" At this point, the other patrons started interacting again.

"What the fuck was that?!" Nigel interjected.

"I'll be honest." The bartender replied in a quiet tone. "they've been like that since after the invasion..."

"Did you actually see the invaders?" Marwood interrupted.

"...yes, I saw them. I saw the death and destruction they brought upon this country. People were begging for their lives, but they were shown no mercy...." The bartender paused. The memories came flooding back. A tear crept down his face. Then followed a few more down the same trail. "...on public display, these people were shot with lasers that caused them to disintegrate..." The bartender put his hand over his eyes to stop the dripping.

Marwood dropped his head in sympathy and put his hand on the bartender's shoulder. "Hey..."

The bartender removed his hand from his face and looked up.

"...they're in a much better place now. I'm sure of it." Marwood replied.

"Yeah." The bartender nodded.

Marwood nodded towards the sentient jukebox. "But they left that behind...?"

The bartender sniffed away his grief slightly. "They said to think of it as a prize for surviving. They really were terrible...all those poor people...suddenly ceasing to exist..."

"But why were you kept alive?"

"It was weird, I didn't even have to beg that much. They said they needed a bartender, and a bar -- so they spared me. They put me to work in this bar and even provided me with these patrons to serve."

"Yeah...what are these patrons exactly? Some kind of alien race?"

"As far as I can tell, they're some kind of android race...they can just power up and down as they please..."

"Interesting...do they tip you well?"

"Reasonably well, actually. Guess that's a perk."

"Wait." Nigel asked. "How does a robot tip?"

"Well, to be honest, I never thought to ask. They just give a lot of change..."

"Are the invaders androids?" Rodney asked.

"Don't think so. If they are, they're doing a damn good job of hiding it."

"You don't sound even remotely French though. What's your story?" Marwood asked.

"I came here on vacation, see. This was before the invasion of course. Nice get-away in Paris I thought -- away from the hustle and bustle of home..."

"...which is where?"

"Texas. Name's Tony by the way."

"Another bartender named Tony..." Rodney whispered to Marwood, hoping this might urge Marwood on with the possibility of coincidence meaning something.

"It's a pretty common fucking name." Marwood whispered back. He paused, spaced out for a second, then came crashing back to reality, with the realization that they had yet to take their drinks.

"Marwood." He reached out and shook Tony's hand, "and these are my accomplices, Rodney and Nigel." Marwood rushed to the tray, grabbed the drinks, and distributed them. "Come on guys, let's not stand on ceremony here..." Marwood murmured hastily. All three slammed them back.

Tony took up the glasses and gave a courteous nod. "Nice to meet y'all. Yeah, the invasion started the morning I was going to fly out, would you believe it. I was in line at the check-in desk and then..."

"These things do happen..."

"Sure, but in this case, they just took away the airport."

"What do you mean, they took it away?"

"One moment I was standing in the airport. Next moment I was standing outside, with everyone around me, still around me and in their exact same positions. It's almost like they managed to somehow negate the structure of the airport without affecting people or their luggage."

"That is very weird." Nigel noted.

It is at this point that four men entered the bar, and the android patrons paused again. Respectively, left to right, they looked like a police officer, an Indian chief, a cowboy and a military man. They each were riding horses and showed no sign of getting off.

"Oh shit!" Tony whispered, then went to hide behind the bar.

"Tony! You here, Tony?" the police officer bellowed. *"Tony?!"*

Marwood walked up to the four horsemen.

"Now, who are you fellas, and what do you want here?"

The policeman got down from his horse. He thrust

his groin in the direction of the jukebox, and lightning emanated from his crotch and connected the two, causing the machine to play "YMCA" by the Village People. Marwood backed away in the direction of his fellow comrades. It is also at this point that the jukebox was seriously thinking about quitting and spending a few weeks in the Mediterranean.

"We are Le Syndicat Flamboyant!" Boomed the Indian chief. At this point, the rest of the men jumped off their horses, and a discotheque ball was lowered completely unsuspended just below the ceiling. One of the horses rolled their eyes and muttered to themselves "Here we go again". The men momentarily struck a masculine pose, before partaking in the song's unique dance routine. Marwood and his men stared at each other in bewilderment.

"What does that mean?" Rodney asked.

"The Flaming Syndicate." Marwood replied. Rodney rolled his eyes.

"Well, they certainly live up to their name. Friends of yours, Marwood?"

"Nope. Haven't a clue who they are."

"Well now, what do you suggest?"

Marwood made a motion towards the door. "I suggest we get out of here, before *we* get struck by lightning."

"Sounds like a good plan."

Nigel perked up. "Wait, let me deal with these guys. After all, I have a gun that I've been dying to use properly." He suggested. Marwood and Rodney tried to stop him, but Nigel already strutted his way over with his hand on his piece, and with the confidence of a man who had more than two balls. He stopped about two feet away.

"Alright, Listen up you loonies! Stop moving your

groins in each other's faces for a second..." Nigel boomed. The music paused.

"It really is quite *offensive.*" Rodney remarked rather sharply, at which point he was hushed by Marwood.

"Not as offensive as *this!*" Nigel said as he took his gun and pointed in the syndicate's general direction, as they stood still, anticipating. *Click.* Nothing happened.

The syndicate laughed at him.

"You call that a gun?" The military man joked. At that instant, the gun disappeared. Nigel backed away at first slowly and then ran to his comrades. The policeman got back on his horse.

"You know, enough of this. They're not worth it. Death will get them in due time. Come on guys, let's invade Germany!" He suggested. They got back on their horses and left. The jukebox went back to its regular playlist, and the androids continued their interactions. Tony resurfaced from his hiding spot, and the discotheque ball faded out of existence, and unbeknownst to everyone there, traveled in time to a period where it felt a bit more appreciated.

Marwood continued his discourse with Tony.

"Were they the invaders?"

"No. Well, not exactly. I didn't see them invade. But they could very well be part of the Associate Group."

"Associate Group?"

"Yeah, they keep an eye on things. Occasionally do the dirty work of the invaders, but not very often."

"Hmmm." Marwood pulled his thinking cap out of his pocket and put it on. It looked like a space helmet.

"How--" Rodney started, before realizing that all Marwood would say is "I'll explain later."

"Tony-how often do these guys come and check on

you?" Marwood inquired.

"Hm...about once every 3 weeks or so."

"Do they have a tracking device on you?"

Tony exposed the back of his left ear, which exposed a microchip.

Rodney interrupted. "OK, so how did you hide from them just now?"

Marwood took his helmet off, folded it up and put it back in his pocket. He smiled at Rodney in a way that conveyed he knew exactly what the answer to that question was but was going to explain it later.

"Well, we'll be off then. Tracking down these invaders. Whatever they look like..." Marwood sighed. Close range laser weaponry on early 21st century Earth. Can't be too many places with that around...

Rodney nudged Marwood. "I thought we were escaping whatever was chasing us in that storm or something. . .?"

"We were. Now though, I realize we should probably chase them back."

Nigel laughed. "You guys are a trip. I've had many a trips myself, but I get the feeling that once I'm done with this, drugs will pale in comparison."

A motorcyclist stopped the men as they exited the bar.

"Excuse me, but have you seen four horsemen riding through here?"

"Uh, yeah." Nigel replied, pointing west of the saloon. "They went that way."

"Thanks," the man answered in an irritated tone. "Bloody typical that is. They always leave me behind. They and their talking horses...have they no respect for more traditional means of transportation?!" He revved his engine. The others remained silent.

"Alright, I guess I'll be off, and catch up with those four hell-raisers. Thanks for the help." With that, the man sped away in pursuit of his sunset-bound companions.

The men looked at each other in a confused manner and shrugged. The remainder of their journey to the van was uninterrupted, except for Marwood, who went back into the bar to take a piss.

"Bloody Boddingtons. Goes right through you, that stuff does." He remarked upon exiting the bar.

"Where are we going?" Nigel asked.

"I say let's go back to my flat. I've got a few things to check on." Rodney suggested.

"Are you sure?" Marwood asked. "We have an invasion to stop, and you want to....check on things?"

"Marwood. It's ...important."

Marwood sighed. They all got in the van, engaged the Tele-Drive and set the coordinates for Rodney's flat.

CHAPTER 4

THE VOYAGE HOME

"*Ladies and gentlemen, this is your captain speaking. We would like to welcome you on board flight DL0042 from Orlando International to London Heathrow. Flight duration is eight hours and twenty minutes currently, and we are expecting a fairly smooth flight today. We hope you enjoy your flight, and thank you for choosing Derivative Airways, a Delta company.*"

Caroline put on her eye mask and sat back in her chair. She reflected on seeing her friends again. Seeing the rest of her family again. Then she thought of Mum and Dad.

"Yes, please tell me about your parents." Caroline opened her eyes, and she was no longer on her flight. She was in a restaurant, and a uniformed gentleman was facing her. She figured he must be the captain of the flight she's on. He poured two glasses of wine.

Caroline's eyes darted around. They definitely were no longer air-bound. But there was quite a bit more amiss, in her mind.

"Where is my family?" There was a sharpness in her voice that could cut titanium. The man looked down at the table and chuckled slightly. "Of course." he thought quietly to himself.

"Your family is safe."

"Oh, good." She paused. "Wait a second." She pinched herself. It hurt.

"You might think you're dreaming."

Caroline sat there paused. She had this innate feeling that she had to listen to every single thing this guy says very carefully. After all, he must be the captain. Right? Fortunately for her, there was no doubt in her mind.

"The thing about dreaming..." He began. "...sometimes, just sometimes, you can never tell. There are an infinite number of tests you can use to try and figure it out. But it's just your brain running mental simulations. The outcome is controlled by your subconscious. Quite an evil thing really." He sipped his wine. Caroline was staring at him, with a morbid fascination in her eyes, as if he was skinning a rabbit right there in front of her, letting its life juice flow out ever so slightly, such that any spillage on the table could be mistaken for a wine stain.

"Evil, because it traps you. You fail the tests, and your brain decides how to punish you for even trying, whilst, in what you perceive as yourself, you're just running. You're trying to survive the chase. Maybe you'll make it. Or maybe you'll be jolted awake the moment you think you don't. Tricky things, dreams are. They are our brain's way of sabotaging ourselves."

"Why are you saying all this? What is your point?"

"My point is, my dear, you need not worry about whether this is a dream or not. I can assure you that soon enough, you will have your proof, but for now, you need to trust me. This is not a dream."

Caroline breathed a sigh. She missed her family. The door opened, causing a draught to run down her spine. An elderly couple stepped in.

"Where is my family exactly?"

"That's...complicated..."

"I have a right to know."

"They're in a parallel universe."

"Parallel universe?"

"Yes. Every time a decision is made by anyone, the options that weren't are
chosen are played out in different universes. Now that isn't the only way a parallel universe is formed, of course--"

Caroline gave a huff of impatience. "So, which parallel universe are they in?"

"PU 131B. Where they are frozen in time due to the physical laws of that particular universe...."

Caroline's expression dropped.

"...but they're safe. I promise!"

"Will I be with them again after we're done here?"

He chuckled again. Of course, at this point, this was the only thing that mattered to her. "Yes. Of course."

Caroline looked towards the corners of the room. Rewinding the conversation in her mind. Making sure everything made sense.

"So, you wanted to know about my parents?" She asked.

He positively grunted at this statement to imply a yes. Caroline sipped her wine.

"Well, they were nice people. They brought up myself and my brother in only what I would consider a normal manner."

"Yes, yes. But what were they like as people?"

"Well, Dad was sharp as a tack. He taught a math course at University College London, as well as doing work in some very high-profile research and development areas, sponsored by massive corporations, so we were a very well to do family..."

"...and your mother?"

"Mum was caring. She always wanted the best. Supported Dad a lot..."

"What happened to them?"

"They died in a car accident about five years ago. Someone in traffic decided to go completely the wrong way..."

"I'm sorry you had to go through that. But listen." He rose. "Come with me,"

"Why?"

"I want to show you something."

He walked towards the window. Like Alice down the rabbit hole, she followed.

--

"So, this yer digs eh, Rods?" Nigel asked as he entered Rodney's apartment.

"Uh, yeah. Mind the mess, would you please." Rodney started as he navigated through the maze of a messy flat.

"Bit squalid for someone of your disposition ain't it? I mean fucking pizza boxen."

"You mean boxes Nigel..."

"No, boxen. Boxes just sound dumb, Rodney."

Rodney, again, thought it was futile to argue the point.

"Look, if you two could just make yourselves at home for a moment, I need to check messages. Kettle's in the kitchen, and teabags are in the small white cylindrical container next to the fridge. In the cupboard above it there are biscuits--"

"Got any Jaffa Cakes?" Nigel asked.

"No--" Rodney replied.

"Here you go." Marwood said, procuring a small tin from his coat pocket.

"Cheers mate." Nigel opened the small tin, grabbed a Jaffa Cake and started nibbling it in a squirrel-like manner.

Rodney looked around his living room, mentally checking that everything was in its place. It was. He mentally checked off Nigel and Marwood, who were now laughing at random YouTube videos on Marwood's laptop. Rodney went into his bedroom to check his voicemail. In accordance with the normal laws of Sol-3 (otherwise known as Earth), answering machines of certain makes and models can just display a digital number which represents how many voicemails one has. Rodney saw the red lining of a square on this display, and though he knew that indeed, it meant he had no voicemails, the fact haunted him. The fact did not haunt him because that meant that no one loved him--no sir. The fact haunted him because today was the day his sister Caroline was meant to arrive home. He checked his watch. She should have been home three hours ago. It wasn't like Caroline to not call. Even a minute's delay in departure or arrival would be a cause for her to call her dear brother and let him know this very minor and ultimately insignificant detail. Rodney, with a sense of seemingly undeserved urgency to those not privy to his family affairs, rushed into the living room.

"God, that David After Dentist kid was well hilarious, God knows what stuff he was trippin' on. C'mon Rodney, you gotta see this shit!" Nigel exclaimed upon noticing Rodney's entrance.

"Nigel, David's going to have to wait--Marwood, can we go to Florida?"

"It's a bit early for that, don't you think? I mean you haven't even met my parents yet-"

"*Marwood!*"

"Oh, heh. Yeah, I guess we can."

"We-We're going to the States?" Nigel asked.

"Yes, Nigel. We need to see what's up with Caroline--"

"Who's Caroline?"

"My sister."

"I see."

"Not yet, but you will once we get there." Marwood commented. The men left the flat in much the same way they entered--in a relatively uneventful fashion.

"I have one more question." Nigel started once they got outside.

"Yes?" Marwood and Rodney simultaneously asked.

"Is this real life?"

Marwood walked up to Nigel, took his sunglasses off and placed a hand on Nigel's shoulder.

"Yes, this is real life, Nigel. We are on our way to save Rodney's sister, because there are strange forces at work in this universe. Now, please, get in the back of the van."

"...sure...Sure thing, boss." Nigel replied. Despite the hypnotism factor, for the first time in a long time, Nigel felt a sense of belonging. This was, in part, due to Marwood, who at least looked and acted like the kind of person who knew what he was doing.

--

As Caroline and the man approached the window, she caught a glimpse of sparkles everywhere.

"I don't care what this guy says, this must be a dream." She thought quietly to herself. As she approached the window, she started to stumble, ever so slightly.

"So, what is your name anyway?" She asked.

He turned around and flashed a small smile. "Matthew." He figured he might as well be straight with her, for once, at least.

"Matthew...so...what you were saying earlier about dreams..."

Matthew raised his eyebrows "Yes?"

"Well, it seemed to me that you are only really concerned with nightmares. That you don't know *real* dreams. The ones that involve snowball fights or walking the dog...."

"...through a grinder?"

Caroline's eyes widened. "No. God, why would you even think that?"

Matthew's gaze went towards the ground. "I'm sorry." He paused and turned his gaze back towards the window. "This is what I wanted to show you." He pointed outward.

There was a great darkness ahead. But it was littered by patches of all colors, greatly lit, moving across the sky and what seemed like the barren landscape in front of them. To Caroline, it seemed that this was the only building in the area for many miles. She supposed that this might not be the case, in which case the case of women's intuition has been spoken for. But she looked out, with genuine curiosity.

"What is this place?" She asked.

"We like to call it Ethereal Space. Part of the Spiritual Realm. What you see here are souls getting transported out to the Universe to become living beings."

Caroline had a puzzled look on her face.

"We are not in the Universe right now. We are technically in a dimension that cannot be perceived by most."

At this point, she figured he was probably not the

captain on the flight. She turned to him.

"How did I get here?"

He turned and looked at her. He supposed her husband was a lucky man. "It's complicated." He replied and turned back.

Caroline shivered. "Don't you feel the cold?"

Matthew smirked. "No. But you're not the first to feel this, so I surmise that maybe it's cold outside." He continued staring towards the outside.

She followed his gaze and could honestly have said that this was the most beautiful landscape she had ever seen. Wanting to take a picture, she reached for her phone, inside her handbag, but it wasn't there.

"Urgh, I must have left my phone on the plane!" She exclaimed. Matthew remained silent, sipping his wine.

Still, she could get it back, she supposed. The sparkling outside caught her attention again. She almost got lost in it. She sighed and felt a weight off her shoulders. Matthew leaned in closer.

"I'm sorry."

"What?"

"About your handbag." Caroline turned around and found that it had disappeared.

"What's happening?"

"You're splitting. Albeit a lot slower than expected. But don't worry this is the good news."

"So, what's the bad news?"

Matthew put his hands on both her shoulders and kissed her on the cheek. "You are still connected to reality, but we need you up here too."

"What do you mean?"

Matthew looked her straight in the eye. "There is a war going on. We need you in both places. You're one of the strongest people out there, so strong that we need to separate your physical body with your soul, in essence having two Carolines to fight the battle."

Caroline looked straight into his eyes, her eyes welling up. "What if I refuse? I have plans you know...I was planning on saving the whales..."

"It's too late. And I'm sorry, but you can't refuse. The wine and the talk of your parents was a spiritual contract you signed, and you've started separating. There's no backing out now."

"Talk of my parents?"

"Yes, we needed you to speak fondly of them...makes the soul easier to coax out."

"What's going to happen to me?!"

Matthew looked towards the floor. "After this is done, I promise you will be reunited with your family..."

She started crying in earnest. *"What's going to happen with me goddammit?"*

He turned to face her. "You're going to wake up on the plane and go home. From there, you will be cared for." He kissed her on the cheek again. *"I promise."*

Caroline burst awake on the plane. "Huh, must have been a bad dream." She thought to herself. But then she looked around and found that her family was still gone. She reached down and found her handbag. Slowly, her hand dragged up the side of the chair, and from there, she rubbed her forehead. After a minute, she tried to fall asleep again, grasping at the possibility that this itself might be a dream. After about half an hour of trying, she gave up, facing the grim reality before her.

CHAPTER 5
BOLLOCKS TO THE UNDERWORLD

It has been noted in various literary and factual works that the universe is a bit on the larger side of things. However, this is only relative to one's position in space, and there exists an entire race of beings that would be the first to point out that the idea that the universe encompasses all of space is indeed incorrect. These people are known as the Popudei, and because of their access to areas of space outside the universe, they get contracted out to all sorts of Planet Creation companies for vast sums of money to sort of keep an eye on things that said company cannot (for reasons that vary from technological limitations of the systems they work with to the fact that everyone went to the pub for Beer-Down Tuesdays). One particular Popudei, who just came from a saloon bar in La Courneuve, France, burst into an office whose door bore the symbol for "Terraine Inc." and addressed Jeff.

"It's the Underworld, sir."

"Thank you, Thrakus, but we already worked that one out. What we're wondering is where that storm came from. It's unusual to see that--"

"I did inquire about that, and they apologized. Shouldn't happen again and they'll be sure to pursue disciplinary action upon the instigator."

"Did you find out why they were doing this?"

"They kept mum about it, sir. I know they are tracking down an individual to aid them, but they specifically said you should keep out of this. You know what those Underworlders are like..."

"Yes, well. They are the ones who sign our paychecks after all..."

"Indeed sir."

"Good work, Thrakus."

"Thank you, sir. Um, also, the Underworld has sub-contracted me to go ahead and help them track down the aforementioned individual..."

"Go ahead."

"Thank you, sir." Thrakus disappeared.

--

"What do you mean it's broken?!" Rodney asked, as they entered The Dog's Bollocks on Royal Phuck Lane. The interior of this bar was not a traditional bar interior, in the way that it completely lacked any kind of subtlety. For starters, the only places to sit on were stools that had seats that looked like testicles, and there were pictures of dogs playing poker--strip poker.

"Well, it is highly experimental technology. They probably haven't figured out how to keep it stable..." Marwood started.

"Well, it is military, Marwood...and you know what they say about military intelligence." Nigel piped in.

"Yes, Nigel, I know, I was in it..."

"I mean all those pointless wars..."

Marwood started to ignore Nigel. "So...can I get anyone a pint or a packet of peanuts or something?"

"I'd rather we figure out a way to find my sister..."

Rodney started.

"Right..." Marwood, again ignoring his friends, turned to the bartender. "Three pints of Guinness, please."

"Guinness, are you sure?" Nigel asked.

"Yes, Nigel--for when we are about to enter the darkest of times that we know, we must drink the darkest of beers."

"Bit ominous, isn't it?" Nigel asked. The beers arrived with a note which read "The time has come..." The subconsciouses of all three men made a small note of this, and their livers started to weep, because they knew what alcoholic hell was awaiting them in the extremely short-term future.

"Drink up, Nige." Marwood solemnly suggested. Marwood then reached into his right trouser pocket and produced a pack of cards, and grinned..."...and now begins the shuffling..."

"Y-what?!" Nigel exclaimed.

"The cards of destiny, my dear Nige. It'll provide some very interesting insights into your future."

Rodney signaled to Nigel to cut it off.

"Hey Marwood..." Nigel placed his arm around Marwood's shoulder. "...why don't we just play some poker?"

Marwood frowned and turned away. He believed in freedom of knowledge, especially the mystical, speculative kind. Nigel turned Marwood back around, with hands on both of his shoulders.

"Look around you, Marwood...this place is meant to have poker played in it." Nigel quietly said. Marwood perked up, and Nigel's eyes bulged slightly. "...but we're all keeping our damned clothes on!"

Marwood laughed.

"So where do we get the chips?" Rodney inquired.

Marwood grinned knowingly and grabbed a small case of poker chips from his back pocket.

"Oh, you're a right deus ex machina, aren't you?" Rodney remarked. They found a nearby table and started a game of poker.

Six hours later, after quite a few games had been played, and more than a few pints had been downed, strange dark brown and dark red circles started appearing on the ceiling of the bar.

"Oh, bloody hell!" Nigel exclaimed. "...not...the Syndicate...ag...again..." Nigel paused, looked at his cards and, with a sinking expression, he flailed back in his chair slightly. "I..." Nigel then leaned forward and slammed his cards down onto the table. "...fold!"

By this point, they were all pretty smashed compared to any normal self-respecting human being, which meant their ability to speak a fully coherent sentence without slurring or repeating was at about five percent capacity. Rodney picked up the ominous note from earlier, which they took with them to the table. He turned it over. It read "Please come outside".

"Hey guys I...err....think..." Rodney was starting to struggle with his words. "...I...think...we should...all...fold...and go outside."

"Wha?" Was Nigel's reply.

"Outside, Nige. We fold the hand ...and go outside. It sez 'ere on dis piss of pepper."

"Pepper? No thanks--I'm not in the mood for spicy food right now...and I have a fucking straight..." Marwood moaned.

"Look guys, just follo' me, willya?"

Marwood frowned and got up. Noticing that Nigel

couldn't rely on his legs to do anything worthwhile, Marwood helped him up.

"Nigel, we...we gotsta...gotsta..." He paused for about twenty seconds; arms locked around Nigel's shoulders. Slowly, they made their way towards the door where Rodney was standing, swaying slightly. A burp occurred at second twelve. "...gotsta...fol...oh...Rod...ney."

Rodney spotted Thrakus standing outside and walked out of the bar.

"Oi!" Rodney exclaimed. "Oi! You! I...know! ...y-you! You were...you were...in frarnse wivuss..."

"Use your words, Rodney..." Thrakus started.

"Hey! How di--"

"I know a lot."

Marwood and Nigel entered outdoors.

"Good evening fellas."

Nigel projectile vomited onto Thrakus.

"Nice to meet you too, Mr. Locosa." Thrakus said as he wiped off the puke with a cloth he procured from his pocket. Upon completion, the cloth simply disappeared into thin air. His jacket still stank to high hell though.

"Oi!" Marwood pointed at Thrakus "You! What's yer name?"

"My name is Thrakus, Marwood."

"Oh."

"Yeah."

"Sorry...about my fr-friend here."

"Yeah, that's ok." Thrakus reached back into his pocket and this time presented a shuriken. It glowed for a second with the result that all became sober, and Thrakus had changed into a new smell-free jacket.

Thrakus got the shuriken at a market over on the planet of Costabom in one of the outer systems. Costabom was rather a brilliant planet. It was basically a planet full of market stalls. Market stalls full of the most wonderful gadgets and devices in the entirety of time and space. They had entry pads that could be configured to any frequency and tunnel in from any dimension. The prices here were high though, so high in fact to warrant the slogan "If it didn't cost a bomb, then it's rubbish compared to what you can get at Costabom: The best time and space has to offer!" It was shortly after they started using this slogan that they immediately had to pull it, among other things to take part in a galactic war, due to the misunderstanding of one of the customers who accidentally caused an act of terrorism by taking the slogan a bit too literally. It was in this post-apocalyptic Costabom, that Thrakus found the shuriken on the "Fuck it, 97% Off" sale. He actually used real money for once, but it really didn't matter since it was marked down so cheaply, it was practically stealing.

Back in the present time, Nigel cradled his own head. His first thought was that a pig took a shit in it. "Oh my God." was his second thought, and as he looked up at Thrakus, he found himself scrambling slightly. "I am so sorry...what was your name again?"

"Thrakus, and you can help pay the cleaning bill for that jacket..."

"Of course." Nigel scrounged around his pocket. "I'm afraid I don't have much change right now."

"Don't worry, you will soon enough, and that's all that matters. You can consider me a patient man."

Nigel and Rodney raised their eyebrows.

"It doesn't matter." Thrakus made a hand gesture like one would usher a small child to quieten down.

"Look, what are you doing here? I keep on finding

these weird notes..." Rodney started.

"Ah, yeah. That was me."

"I see."

"Quite."

Rodney raised his right eyebrow. "You didn't answer my question."

Thrakus smirked. "I'm here to take you to the Underworld."

At this point, Marwood stood up straight and saluted. "Ready when you are, sir."

"B...but...what--" was about all Rodney could muster. The drinking and time lapse had paid its toll as he forgot the obvious reply which followed.

"I'll explain later."

"Alright fellas, hold onto your horses." Thrakus instructed. He lifted a boulder from his pocket, which Rodney mentally noted as like the way Marwood pulled out his thinking cap. Thrakus closed his eyes, put his hands over the boulder and gave the impression he was pretending to type on it.

"Yo, what in the name of dumb shit is going on here?!" Nigel exclaimed before Marwood gently elbowed him in the ribs, just enough as to not make him throw up again.

"It's an ancient ritual. *DON'T* interrupt." Marwood whispered sharply.

After about five seconds, the boulder started to glow. Then a blue glowing circle on the ground encompassing the party appeared, and Thrakus stopped his typing imitation, and opened his eyes. Everything in the circle started to dematerialize.

--

One thing that could be said about the Underworld is that it was very red. It is a popular notion that the

Underworld is a very dark place with plenty of screaming and torturing going on. This is simply wrong. The truth is, the Underworld is actually a very well-lit place due to all the abundant fire. As for the screaming and torturing, this was mostly on the part of the lawyers, as the rulers of the Underworld (of which there were many, far more than what would be considered regular size for a governing body) tried to find as many legal loopholes as humanly (or rather, *inhumanly*) possible, in the many contracts they had with the world above as well as many other worlds.

The four men all materialized, all falling to the floor from the shock of there being something actually solid to stand on. The travel process they undertook possessed the very same gravitational laws they were used to, but they weren't really standing on anything substantially solid. It was quite soothing and really quite liberating. As for the visuals around them, it seemed to resemble a vortex of kinds, and since all the men had at one point seen science fiction from the 1980s, none of the men so much as flinched at the sight. This was a pity, since the Underworld was all about impressing their visitors, but having been out of touch with current Earth culture for the last forty years or so, they totally failed to keep up with their sci-fi spook-out standards.

After some initial groaning, they rose to their feet.

"So, this is Hell?!" Nigel exclaimed.

"Actually, Nigel, I believe they call it the Underworld." Rodney replied. "It seems people around here get very offended if you call it Hell."

"Alright, Dave?" A grubby voice said from a distance.

"Who the fuck is Dave?" Nigel asked.

"I dunno..." Rodney replied, his eyes darting around,

while his brain thought *"Not this shit again."*

At this point, Marwood stretched his arms and took a deep breath. "Aahh...the underworld! 'twas like I never left!"

Nigel and Rodney stared at the man like he was gouging out the eyes of chickens and devouring them.

"What?" Marwood inquired.

Rodney walked over very calmly and put his hand on Marwood's shoulder.

"I think you owe Nigel and I some explaining."

"Yeah, I guess you're right. Very well. But you are not going to like it."

"Marwood, we've seen some pretty fucking crazy shit already. I don't think there's anything you can say now that'll shock us--"

"...and if there is, we can just smoke later and just chalk it all up to getting high!" Nigel interjected. Rodney gave him a sharp shut-up gaze.

"...anyway, so yeah. we're all here for the long haul now..." Rodney continued.

"OK..." conceded Marwood and pointed out a nearby table and chairs. They all sat down. An infernal being approached them. The only thing to say that he was infernal were the small horns on either side of his temples. Also, he had the tan that could only be had by someone with almost constant exposure to fire.

"Hello gentlemen, and welcome to Hell's Grill! Your one stop for grilled and barbeque from the Underworld's best." The being greeted the group. "Today's soup of the day is the Hot Soul Soup, and our special, directly imported from PU-154 is the Eager Beast Stew with our special homemade side of lawyer fritters." He handed out menus to everyone. "Can I get anyone a drink?"

Nigel and Rodney turned ghost-white and briefly stared at each other before staring back at the waiter. Marwood spoke.

"Can I get three tequila sunrises, and maybe about half an hour before we order..." He leaned in, to whisper to the waiter "...these guys have never been here before, and they seem a bit shell-shocked--"

Marwood paused for a split second. "Actually, better make that three tequila shots instead. Something a bit stiffer to soak up the atmosphere."

"Oh, I totally understand sir." The waiter whispered back and then stood up to compose himself. "We have a particularly wonderful and *lively* house tequila! You'll love it! If you need anything, just holler! Name's Tony." He wandered back into the kitchen.

Rodney thought for a moment. He had vague memories of his grandmother saying to him when he was young that he should never ignore coincidences that occurred three times or more. Unfortunately, it was so vague that Rodney passed it off as something that happened either in a dream or when he was drunk.

CHAPTER 6

BLOODY HELL

Deep within the bowels of the Underworld, there was a burp. One unfamiliar with the ways of the Underworld would assume that this was a regular noise, because the construct from which it emitted would appear alien to those outside the realm of planetary management. Planetary management has one very basic principle: to keep life flowing. Indeed, the Counsel for Planetary Management won't even give a basic license to organizations that fail to provide a means of reincarnation for the dominant lifeforms on the planet an organization intends to manage. However, if an organization gets the basic license, the Counsel grants upgraded licenses to those who can reincarnate more basic lifeforms, and to those organizations that can provide planetary defense services. The Underworld has met all of the aforementioned requirements, and thus have the most advanced license the Council can bestow upon an organization: A Tier I License, which also grants a two way access to a Spiritual Realm, where spirits can reside until they are assigned to new life, affording the Underworld the luxury of just being a management office. In the planetary management world, only fifteen organizations have managed to acquire these, so this is nothing to sniff at. The burp, however, was an indication that things were not normal.

Within the dark recesses, a large bottle of tequila lay in wait. The bottle itself felt rather depressed. Mere weeks ago, it was being poured for all sorts of drinks -- shots, on the rocks, even mixed with orange juice and grenadine (which it enjoyed the most -- the grenadine was very sweet on it), but recently, the drinking of tequila had stopped, as the drinking of harder liquors increased (compared to some infernal liquors, tequila was very much a lightweight). And thus, when Tony entered the chamber from which darkness dwelled, and picked up the bottle of tequila, the bottle of tequila was so excited to be used that it would have pissed itself, had it the capability to do so.

Tony brought to the table the bottle of tequila (who, were it not for physical limitations, would not be able to contain itself at this point), and three shot glasses. Marwood insisted he would pour the shots himself, and thus Tony left the table, and ventured into the kitchen to teach some rather terrible lawyers what it truly meant to be *terrifried*.

Marwood sniffed the air curiously and looked around.

"Something's wrong." He licked his finger and pointed it to the air. The fact that it didn't dry instantly gave him cause for concern.

The other two glared at him.

"No shit. The fuck are we here for anyway. Marwood?!" Nigel eyed his surroundings, as if he was meant to be there in secret. "Let's at least take the shot."

"Yeah..." Marwood trailed off. "To..."

They all paused and tried to think of a toast. At this point, a very scrawny being ran towards them.

It was rather tall, very thin and its skin was grey. Its mouth was very strange looking, mostly because of its lips being green and sideways. It had red beady eyes and was dressed in military attire. It also possessed ten fingers on each hand.

"Mister Marwood, sir! Private letter for you!" The being gave Marwood the letter and then saluted with its left hand. Nigel's eyes widened.

"At ease, private." Marwood directed. "You may be dismissed."

"Thank you, Mister Marwood, sir!" The being zoomed off into the darkness. Nigel turned to his right side and threw up on the infernal pavement. The other men budged slightly with widened eyes.

"Y'alright, Nige?" Rodney asked.

"The...the...thing...sideways   lips...ten   fingers...I..." Nigel paused and raised his hand, giving the other two warning that he may, indeed, vomit once more.

"...I don't think I can take this anymore." And thus, a fountain of yellow vomit was expelled from his mouth.

Marwood summoned Tony. "Can I please get some water here quick."

"Of course, sir!"

Rodney straightened himself up a bit, thinking he was probably the only normal one among them. He was, of course, not exactly right. No one who enters the underworld in the fashion that they did lead a life that was anywhere close to the books.

"Just breathe Nigel..." Rodney instructed.

In. Out. In again. And out again. Slowly and calmly, with Rodney's almost hypnotic tone of voice and guiding hand, Nigel regained his sense of control. The glass of water came, and Nigel nursed it.

"Maybe we should leave the shots for later..." Rodney suggested.

"Bollocks to that!" Marwood replied.

Rodney paused and stared at Marwood.

"...you haven't read what I've just read." and with that, Marwood downed all three shots. "Come on --" Marwood started as he rose swiftly from his seat. " --We need to go! Follow me."

--

The general felt very much at home in his office. He started out as a lowly private all those years ago, back in a more innocent time. Life had been so easy back then, he reminisced. Now he gets more-or-less whatever he wants, but it was more stressful now, not to mention times are more dangerous, what with the recent invasion. Oh, yes, the invasion. At first, it was just the Parasites, but those were easy to contain. Basic pest control, really. But then they started to bring in reinforcements, unrelenting -- bringing in their friends from the other side of the galaxy, the Gang of Leathers. A brutal kind they are -- blowing up entire planets, just to record it all and upload it to the ether for the entertainment of all Leatherkind. And as soon as it caught wind that they were involved, a planet on the outer reaches of the universe by the name of Sophos, homeworld of the Maybes, joined in. The general knew at this point, there wasn't much hope. Malevolent factions spanning the entire universe had gathered and he could stand to lose everything. He felt the weight of existence itself rested upon his shoulders. That was why he had to pull out all the stops. That was why he had to contact Marwood.

A woman in a police uniform and mud-brown eyes

slowly waltzed into the general's office and closed the door.

"He'll never come, you know." She cooed softly.

"Well." The general paused. His back to her, he was staring out into the black-red sky that his window exhibited. The Underworld at night. It was almost comforting, knowing how guarded the place is. Almost. Unfortunately for him, he knew all too well exactly how guarded, and he knew it was not enough. He looked at the glass in his hand, which contained some rather expensive whisky he brought in case the end days were to happen. He swirled it slightly, sipped, and then smirked, thinking that his fate, and indeed, the fate of all the universe, would be better off swirling into a black hole than dealing with this shit. Sighing, he took a sip, and straightened himself up again. "I had to take the chance." The general said firmly.

"Mmm...tell me, General, how many ships are recorded to have left Sophos?"

"Impossible to tell." He stared down at the whisky again. Swirl, sip, smirk. Faster this time, and this sip went down a little rougher, leaving his vocalization to be temporarily grittier, ever so slightly. "You know that. You know what they're like."

"An impossible situation. And You know what they say about impossible situations...."

He stared slightly higher into the ether of the Underworld, even though there was nothing to see, as if he were trying to recall a memory. He failed. That was new. The rules had changed. Swirl, sip, smirk. "What do they say?" He asked, still entranced by the night of the ethereal abyss.

"They say they turn me on." The woman walked

towards him, throwing her police hat at a coat stand. The velocity at which she threw the hat caused the stand to sway slightly, before giving into the gravitational pull of the ground. The noise of the collision broke the general out of his trance, and he turned around.

"Now Luciel, this is hardly the time for..." She placed an index finger upon his lips.

"Hush, General. The universe is ending. Some say it already has and that we're just waiting for time itself to catch up. And even if that isn't the case...the Maybes, well, their impossibility fields can never be..." She arched her back, letting out a slight moan. "...penetrated." His eyes widened, as to be expected, and she relaxed. "Now I did what you said and directed your man to you. I have come for my payment." She removed the fingers and gave the general a passionate, but brief, kiss. "General Courtney, the end of the universe has come, and I want you to fuck me."

"But what about Marwood?"

"Use a time field."

"I can't do that; we'd both be detected."

"I meant on us, not him." Setting time fields remotely can be easily traced, as they leave fragments of time energy that can be picked up by any sort of metal detector and certain breeds of dog.

"Oh hmm, good idea." General Courtney pressed a couple of buttons on his desk, surrounding the office in a time field, nothing can get in or get out. In this case, the general and his rather handy mistress stay in the office as they get down to the rather important matter of...payment of services, but to everyone else, the office would be empty, and anyone would be none the wiser. At this point, it had slipped General Courtney's mind that

Marwood wasn't just anyone.

Marwood and the gang approached the office.

"It's empty." Rodney observed.

"Of course it's empty! There's a lot of official top-secret work that goes on here. Can't afford to let secrets out down here." Marwood explained. He started fiddling with his watch.

"Oi, boss, what're you doing?" Nigel inquired.

"I'm setting the time." And with that, a green aura surrounded the office. Luciel and General Courtney appeared half-dressed and were sharing a cigar. Once it registered in their brains that there were people looking at them, their eyes widened. Rodney looked quizzically at Luciel, recognizing her as the woman in the dream that ultimately brought him here, and then their eyes just beamed at each other for a moment. Luciel then turned towards General Courtney.

"I'm sorry I must go." Said Luciel, and she left quite literally, in a flash.

"Who was that?" Nigel asked.

General Courtney took the cigar out of his mouth and threw it away. His cigar smoking moment was ruined, though he showed no concern for it. "A...friend. Of sorts."

Marwood looked at Courtney and grinned. "General, eh? Bloody hell mate, you really made it. I remember when you were a corporal fighting the good fight. And now you get to sit in an office all day. Still..." Marwood paused, shaking his head slightly. "...the pressure must get to you."

"Ah...well, yes, sometimes. You see that's why I..." The General noticed that Marwood was fiddling with his watch again. "...what are you doing?"

"Protecting us." Marwood replied.

"From what?"

"Christian Lucifer."

"That renegade bastard, he couldn't get in here. There's layers of security."

"I'm sorry, general, but all that security? Disarmed."

"How can you possibly tell?"

Marwood smiled. "Let's just say intuition."

"Bullshit. I don't take that crap from anyone. Not even you!"

"General, if I told you everything, you know what the consequences would be."

"The universe is about to end, I'm sure spilling a few secrets wouldn't hurt."

Marwood took a cigar off Courtney's desk, lit it and started smoking it. "Oh Courtney, so innocent. You always were."

"What?"

"Well, ok, I can tell you one secret, but that's it."

"What's that?"

"There's more to space than just the universe." Marwood grinned and then pressed a couple of buttons on his watch and the office was surrounded in a time field. Fortunately, being alien technology, there were extra settings one had to put in to let the field pick up humans, but unfortunately, Marwood was working with outdated software. Left behind was one lonely soul -- and the lights just went out.

"Hello?" A whimper started. "Where did everyone go? Courtney? Marwood?"

"Hello old friend." Said a rather grim voice. He put a blade to the man's chin.

"Who goes there?" The whimpering continued. "I

promise I'm armed."

"It's...'Biker Greg'."

"Oh, Greg mate! Great to see you again. Well, maybe not under these circumstances, but maybe you'll buy some more Charlie?"

"Eh, no. I got all the drugs I need. But I do need...an assistant. Someone who can be a bit dodgy when needed. You up for it?"

Nigel paused for a moment.

"Tell you what. If you're not, I'll slash your throat."

Nigel started laughing.

"Death is no laughing matter unless you're the religious sort. Are you religious?" Christian asked.

Nigel's laughter died down a bit, but he was still grinning. "In a place like this, I don't need to be."

Christian Lucifer grunted, let out a massive battle cry and slashed Nigel's throat, eventually cutting his head off. Blood splattered everywhere.

"Ah, human blood. Can't beat it." Christian said as he licked a bit of Nigel's blood off his blade. He turned around, and proceeded to leave, not noticing that Nigel died with a smile upon his face.

INTERLUDE
A COLD KICK IN THE FAMILY JEWELS

There exists within the universe, regions that are climatically different from one another. The Rordanic Sector is generally considered one of the coldest in the universe. It was here, on the planet of Califahn, in the Gardens of Timideaux, that King Crotin witnessed the first steps of his child, Thurlowe.

"I am so proud. First steps...next thing you know, he'll be in command of the whole empire!" Exclaimed Crotin to Kanthor, one of his shadowed advisors, who stood by his side.

"Indeed sir, but you need to be careful. You know how hard it is to rule well in this sector of the universe." Kanthor replied. "Remember the war with your brother."

Crotin nodded and grunted in acknowledgement. Winter had already come, and night was dawning. Crotin, even in his royal red robes, started to shiver as the temperature dropped. Kanthor just stood there, in his usual attire, consisting of a black and cream striped robe, and a dark purple hood. Cold like this never bothered Kanthor; he had seen much worse.

Advisors were essential to rulers in the Rordanic Sector, since the cold gave rulers a disposition for corruption. The advisors were picked for their sense of secrecy; they had to be trusted, and they needed...well, a universal sense about them. In most cases, they were former galactic vicars, having seen the way worlds were ran, and being privy to the most notorious -- and indeed most shocking -- of confessions and calls for advice from all sorts of people, from the likes of soldiers on the front line having seen the worst destruction laid upon their companions to the village adulteress who fucked the A/C guy, when her husband was at work (the husband in question ended up strangling the family cat when he found out. The advisor who heard about it was shocked by this, but only because there was no need for A/C in the Rordanic Sector).

Many years later, around the Earth Age of 22, Thurlowe left for his required military duty. He was stationed in one of the outer regions of The Rordanic Sector, taking part in the war against a renegade race of highly intelligent entrepreneurial pirates called The Appearers.

The Appearers actually did not name themselves as such -- in fact, they were too busy in their formative years as a society to ever come up with a name for themselves -- they simply referred to themselves as "Us" or "Ourselves". They were called The Appearers because when they appeared, everything they wanted disappeared (which then reappeared in their loot hulls, heavily guarded by quantum henchmen).

The war against The Appearers came to a dark and bitter end, and Califahn, amongst many other planets in the Sector, fell to them. Thurlowe, who was of royal blood, who was told from a young age that he would achieve greatness, had failed. He had failed his people, who had counted on him to protect them after his parents were slain by The Appearers in their elderly slumber during the early days of the war.

He had also failed himself, blaming himself for the deaths of many. In some of the more rustic sectors, he would have committed suicide, but in the cold winds of the Rordanic Sector, he considered revenge for himself, and his people against The Appearers.

In the underground shelters of Califahn, one of the few places The Appearers would allow socialization amongst those who survived, Thurlowe, who now looked much like a beggar from the streets of New York -- making him indistinguishable from the rest of his people -- met with his father's primary adviser at the local watering hole (the Appearers would never deny booze to even their worst enemies. In fact, alcohol poisoning was a popular execution for their prisoners). Kanthor was still dressed in the very same shadowed and regal attire he wore the last time Thurlowe saw him as a child.

"Hello Kanthor" Thurlowe greeted.

"Thurlowe. Good to see you survived." Replied the monotonous Kanthor.

"Yes, well. Good to see you survived too. In fact, you look just the same as you did when I was a mere child."

"Must be the clothes."

Thurlowe slightly raised an eyebrow. "Really?"

"That and...us advisors age well."

"Surely, being an adviser is just your job?"

Kanthor's bright blue eyes stared at Thurlowe, making direct eye contact -- not to inspire fear per se, but "to let the wonder of his agelessness settle into his consciousness" as Kanthor's associates would refer to it.

"Oh." Was all Thurlowe could muster.

"Listen, kid --"

"I'm not a kid! Everyone says that, but I'm not a kid. Kids don't ever let destruction reign on their people like that!"

"That's not something you can blame yourself for. You were defending us with the best of our galactic fleet!"

A single tear crept down Thurlowe's face, as he gazed upon a portrait on the back wall of the last king and queen of Califahn, which used to hang in his father's office, and now just hung in this pub. The picture was salvaged; slightly beaten up, but still in one piece.

"I never got to say goodbye." He said softly, barely able to hold himself together.

Kanthor placed a hand on Thurlowe's shoulder. "You know, it's just the Effect right now. You go to bed -- tomorrow you'll be right as rain."

The Effect was a weekly planetary alignment issue. Normally a year is defined in terms of an orbit of a planet around a major star. For Califahn, this occurs weekly (and they arbitrarily decided that 52 such orbits would constitute a year). On the day some would call Tuesday, a satellite that is directly in the line of Califahn zaps the planet with temporary rays that heightens emotion. No one on Califahn knows who put it there, but wars over the last couple of centuries have gotten in the way of any attempts to destroy it.

Thurlowe woke up in a cold sweat and went down to the chapel to pray. There, he saw a vicar -- an old Califahnian with long green hair, which was a holy tradition. Thurlowe knelt in front of a shrine, upon which small statues of a man and a woman stood, lowered his head, and closed his eyes. The vicar overheard Thurlowe's prayer:

"Dear The GrandMother and The GrandFather, I ask

that you look upon the spirits of the long-lost king and queen of this dear planet, Califahn. It's been a while since we've spoken, I know -- I kept on thinking things would get better, but I realize now that I was a fool to do so --"

The vicar placed his hand on Thurlowe's shoulder sympathetically. Thurlowe's head rose, with eyes still closed. His nerves heightened, however, causing his voice to shake.

"-- I want to leave this place, GrandMother, and GrandFather; I have had enough. I need a new life. Everything about this place reminds me of my parents and how much worse things have gotten." Thurlowe took a deep breath. "Amen and may the Gardens of the Sky World bear you many fruits!" Thurlowe opened his eyes, stood up and gave the shrine a traditional salute.

You'd be mistaken to think that the vicar hated words with the manner that Thurlowe spat them out, his voice stamping them into the surrounding air. "It's a pity you're gay." The vicar mumbled.

Thurlowe turned around and gave the man a quizzical look. "What do you mean by that?"

"I mean, my dear Thurlowe, that the sadness for your parents' death and your passion for vengeance are exactly the kind of thing the girls around here are looking for."

"It's nothing I can help--"

"Of course not, my dear boy. No more than you can help grieving your parents' death."

"What's your point?"

The vicar shrugged. "I am an old vicar, my dear boy. Sometimes I have no point."

Thurlowe grunted.

"But I do know some things about this life that may help."

"This life?"

The vicar raised his eyebrows.

"You mean to say there's more to living than just this one life we have?"

The vicar laughed. "Oh, my dear boy, there are many people in this city wiser than I who can help you answer that question."

"Doubt it. I mean you are the vicar!"

"Being vicar is just my job. I am so much more than that."

"What do you mean?"

The vicar beckoned Thurlowe to follow him and they took a seat in the front pew. Above them was a large dome-shaped window. He pointed at the starry night sky.

"Out there--" The man started. "All of those stars out there--billions of them. Do you really think it was one man and one woman who created it all?"

Thurlowe didn't know how to reply to this. He was hypnotized by the Vicar's suggestion. Inspired, even.

"I mean yes--" The vicar continued. "--it is what I preach. I preach that The GrandMother and GrandFather created and maintained the universe from the Gardens of the Sky World. But I'll tell you a little secret, boy." He leaned into the boy's ear, whispering "I think there's a lot more to it than just that." The old man pulled back and grinned. Thurlowe thanked him for his time and walked out of the chapel.

The next morning, Thurlowe was called to The Office. The Office resided at the top of the highest skyscraper in Califahn. Thurlowe remembered the legend that surrounded this particular skyscraper. When he was a child, it was called the Head Chapel, named such because the "head" of the chapel rose so high into the sky, it was said to have contact with the Sky World, and thus the word and wishes of the GrandMother and the GrandFather came straight through the building itself. When the Appearers came, and saw the momentous building, they decided to use it as the center for their business dealings with off-planet establishments. The Office was on the highest floor accessible in the building, floor 456, which sat just beneath the clouds.

Accompanied by the Elder Guards of the Appearers, Thurlowe entered The Office with his head hung low. The Office could be likened to a five-star hotel room. Except that the Appearers were a race of pirates with always something better to do, too proud to send anyone to deal with something they thought of as rather private, and thus the en-suite bathroom looked like it had seen much better centuries. The Appearers, however, currently had 23 planetary races in their possession, the most recent of which were a race of wolf men called the Fon, on the waterfall-laden forest moon of Barrze. Around the time just after the conquering and suppression of the Fon, Appearean scientists developed a technology called the Evolution Bomb. The Evolution Bomb was an artificially intelligent device to create new self-eliminating species within an ecosystem in a way that goes completely unnoticed by whatever life-form they're programmed to be against. At least that was the militaristic reason for their existence. They work in clusters, and each one scans the surroundings and lifeforms of the area it's dropped in, sharing this data to other Evolution Bombs on the same surface, rather like a social network. They then decide amongst themselves, first coming up with all lifeforms they could evolve, then weigh the tradeoffs with the data they have at hand, eliminating some possibilities, and then taking a vote on the remaining ones. In the case of the ones that Billson, Chief of the Appearers, used for his own private purposes, they took into account the canine genetics of the Fon and the fresh greenery of Barrze.

Just as Thurlowe and the guards entered The Office, Billson was leaving said en-suite bathroom, opening a cage of freshly scented puppies into the bathroom, and locking the door behind them.

"A whole cage, my lord?" One guard asked.

Billson blushed slightly. "It...was a doozy. Might not want to go in there until it is once again..." He turned and grinned and flashed a grin containing only a few teeth. "...fresh." He then made eye contact with Thurlowe, and instantly had his clothes changed out by nano-ants from looting gear into something closer to business professional. He motioned Thurlowe over to the desk, which sat behind red velvet curtains, keeping out the light that Califahnians considered holy at that altitude.

"Come, Thurlowe, have a seat."

The guards closed the entrance to The Office and stood by the door. Thurlowe took his seat in front of Billson, looking at the floor the whole time, thinking they might as well have had him in handcuffs, even though they had no intention of doing so. Billson had his back turned, facing the red curtain he personally picked out for The Office.

"As you may know, Thurlowe, the Appearers have many lines of business..."

"Yes." Thurlowe paused. "Sir."

Billson looked up at the curtain rod. He remembered watching the tree he approved to chop down just for that one piece and shed a tear. He wiped it away, and turned to

Thurlowe, making direct eye contact.

"This planet of yours--"

"Califahn."

"Yes. We have this tower..."

Thurlowe kept his mouth shut.

"What I'm saying, Thurlowe, is that..." At this point, Billson put his palms upon the desk, squeezing his eyes, trying to hold back the tears, thinking about how to break the news. "...we've decided to leave your planet, in favor of more prosperous business opportunities in other galaxies."

Thurlowe lifted his head and having played poker a lot during his time in the military, managed to keep expressionless.

"Therefore Thurlowe." Billson said with words weighing him down, as if they were skyscrapers themselves. "Being the rightful heir to the throne, as per Appearean Law, you are allowed to rule your land again as you see fit. On one condition."

"What's that?"

"That we leave one responsible party behind. Consider it a parting gift. A souvenir, if you will."

"And who is that?"

Billson turned towards the curtain and pulled his pants up in a very dominating way.

"Well, to be honest, we thought this planet could do with some help...considering that this building is the only real redeeming quality. I'm sure you've heard of our Evolution Bomb project..."

Thurlowe acknowledged with a nod. At this point, there were yelps and explosions coming from the bathroom. Billson snapped his fingers and widened his eyes.

"Ah! I believe the bathroom is now ready for use!" Billson bellowed. As he motioned for the guard to the left of the door. "You! Go check it out!" The guard dutifully went towards the bathroom door and opened it. What greeted him was an overwhelming bright green light and a scent as fresh as the mountains. The guard exited the bathroom and nodded at Billson, confirming that the puppy operation was a success. Billson turned back towards Thurlowe without missing a beat.

"Anyway, Thurlowe, we're leaving here our chief scientist on that project."

"Which is who?"

Billson turned to Thurlowe, with a sparkle in his eye, and a grin, that, if mapped on the layout of the Earth, would be as wide as Asia.

"His name is Christian Lucifer. Real bright fella!" He bellowed then lessened his grin slightly. He turned back to his curtain. "Anyway, Thurlowe, good riddance to you." And with that, the guards came and threw Thurlowe out of the building. Within a week, the Appearers had left, thus leaving Thurlowe rightfully as King of Califahn. And though there were celebrations abound throughout the entire planet, Thurlowe, however, never forgave, and he never forgot.

CHAPTER 7

BLASTS FROM THE PAST (AND ONE FROM THE CONTINUOUS)

Thrakus breathed; The air was fresh, pure as a virgin's lips. The wind blew a light breeze. Waterfalls flowed and gushed into rivers of crystal blue waters. Butterflies flew among fields of rose-tinted grass, and the five suns of Centarus hung in the sky, lighting up a planet whose civilization had fallen. They had all been wiped out in this, the great war. The dominant race had died out, but nature carried on. Out from the wind, Luciel appeared -- She walked through a field of purple poppies towards Thrakus.

"You know, life was different before the war..." She started.

Thrakus grunted.

"You were different before the war." Luciel continued.

"We're both popudeis. Technically, we could go back."

"Yes, but you know we really shouldn't, seeing as we're both public servants. Anyway, knowing what happens, happens anyway, could you really be happy?"

Thrakus sighed. "That's the problem with you, Luciel. You're too concerned with the future."

"The only way to live is to look forward, and as popudeis, we have a special ability to look forward. Hell, we can just enter a different universe if we wanted to...under normal circumstances, anyway."

Thrakus put his finger on her lips. "Shhh." He said softly. As he removed his finger, he knelt down, picked up a green rose and sniffed it. "There are certain advantages to being in the present, though."

"What's that?"

Thrakus smirked. "Well, take right now for instance. There's you and me, here in this beautiful place. Civilization is dead, so there's no one to disturb..."

Luciel grinned. "I thought you'd never ask."

--

Rodney woke up. As his eyes started to re-focus, he found himself on the floor of a nightclub.

"Oh, thank god, it was all a dream." was his first thought, as he started to get up.

Once he had fully gotten ahold of himself, he approached the bar for some water. He downed a glass and approached the dance floor for some movin' action. At first, he was awkward, but before long, he joined a conga line around the pink elephant in the middle of the room. However, the elephant started stomping its feet and blowing its trunk violently, before finally exploding into a cloud of metaphor. Everyone cheered as the elephant went out with a bang, expelling vast amounts of pink and lemon-yellow confetti from within. Everyone except Rodney, who, still feeling thirsty, was now scanning his surroundings. "Drat" he thought to himself "The barman disappeared." And with that, he ran out of the club. Upon exiting, he found Marwood standing by the wall near the entrance, smoking what looked like a cigarette, except that the burning end was bright blue. This little fact had totally failed to impress Rodney, as he embarked onto more pressing matters.

"I knew it was you!" Rodney exclaimed.

"Course it was, mate. I take care of you, you know that."

Rodney grabbed Marwood by the collar. "Take care of me?! You made me hallucinate a bloody pink elephant in the middle of the dancefloor!"

Marwood smirked at him. "That was no hallucination, Rodney. That elephant was there to party down. It has one purpose in life, to act as an emergency conga line assist. Once the conga gets going, its purpose in life is done."

Rodney let go. "That must be alien technology!"

Marwood took a puff. "From your point of view, perhaps, but not from theirs."

"Marwood, what are you saying? We're not on Earth?"

Marwood took another puff and exhaled. "Far from it, Rodney. Millions of light years, maybe even billions. Where we are, it's difficult to tell at this point."

"Why?"

"Because you and I need to have a little chat, Rodney."

"About what?"

"Life, and the universe." Marwood paused "...but not everything."

"Why not?"

"Possible copyright infringement, and we don't want that -- the universe is in enough trouble as it is."

They found a park bench nearby and sat down. Rodney looked up at the sky. It was littered with stars and contained three moons -- one silver and two yellow. They made a perfect isosceles triangle if you were to draw an imaginary line between them, which wasn't hard to do in this case, since they were firing lasers between one another.

"What's going on there?" Rodney asked.

"Wh--" Marwood looked up to where Rodney was signaling. "Oh. Trade dispute."

"Trade dispute?"

"Yeah...long story...I'll tell you later."

Rodney raised his eyebrows. "Is it an interesting story?"

Marwood squinted, like he was looking for something specific. "Politically, yes. Particularly, no."

"Oh." Rodney looked disappointed. His first time on a truly alien planet and this is how he is treated. Marwood sighed.

"Where's Nigel?" Rodney asked.

"In the Underworld, where we left him."

Rodney at this point was at a loss for words, so he gave Marwood the kind of look an abused puppy would give its owner, with an unsubtle hint of anger. Marwood's eyes widened as he continued.

"We had to get out of there, Rodders. Our lives were threatened."

"But Nigel...was somehow a necessary casualty?!"

"Rodney...look. I try my best with what I have..." He paused and looked Rodney straight in the eye, " ...and that's extremely alien technology. So alien, in fact, that it hasn't even been seen by a human, let alone used on one."

"Marwood, what do you mean? I saw it."

"Yes, Rodney, you did." Marwood paused again. "Do you remember anything from your childhood?"

"Yes, a large part of it. Got bullied a lot at school. Was always dubbed the weird kid."

"...and you got into that biking accident when you were five years old..."

"...I was biking down the street, and all of a sudden hit a lamppost at what must have been five miles an hour. Had to get air-lifted to the hospital."

"Do you remember waking up?"

"Yeah, there were bright lights. Bright neon green lights. Then I saw Mum, Dad, and Caroline." Rodney's eyes squinted as he remembered.

"Rodney, you weren't going five miles an hour, you were going much faster. A speed that no human can survive."

Rodney entered stunned silence.

"Rodney, you were part of an alien adoption program, as was your sister Caroline."

Rodney stayed inside the state of stunned silence.

"Don't worry, we were cognizant enough to keep the alien part away from humans."

Marwood took a cigar out of his pocket and lit it. He started smoking. Rodney started remembering more.

"My doctor -- Doctor Somerfield -- he looked like a younger version of you--"

"It *was* a younger version of me."

Rodney ignored him and carried on reminiscing. "Just as whacky too. When I was three years old with a cold, he would bribe me with bourbon biscuits to get better and give me this great ridiculous grin."

"Bourbon biscuits act as a cure for common ailments for your species."

"But then he died..."

"Smoke and mirrors. To protect you."

Rodney went silent. He had a feeling he missed something. Then it hit him like a golden brick dangling in mid-air.

"That doctor was you, wasn't it?"

Marwood took a puff of his cigar and grinned. "Rodney, I always take care of you, remember? I had to make sure you were okay. More than okay in fact. Had to make sure you were spectacular."

"Why?"

"Because there's a war going on..." Marwood took another puff, turned to Rodney, and put his hand on his shoulder "...and we're going to end it." Marwood stubbed out his cigar on the ground.

"Come, follow me."

They got up and followed the walking trail to a nearby river. Marwood fiddled with his watch and spoke into it: "Somerfield ready at the point." At this point, a spacecraft materialized in the sky as if it had been lying in wait. The ship was vast; it could have housed entire civilizations, which was why it often invoked its own cloaking device -- to prevent any inquisition from interested, malevolent parties. Rodney had about three seconds to think "Now, this is more like it..." before his system got overloaded and he fainted, as the ship beamed the men up.

The men materialized inside a dark and spacious room. They were greeted by what looked like human members of the crew who looked rather puzzled at Rodney. Marwood dusted himself off.

"Don't worry about him. He doesn't remember." Marwood remarked.

A man dressed in a bright green robe came forward. The robe had gold markings all over it, which to any human would seem random. They are, in fact, the markings of a high priest who has passed through the trials of the Moral Academy on Rushmore.

"...but he will remember. He must remember." Said the man.

"Yes, Dorius. I know."

--

Thrakus lay naked in the blue grass with Luciel, also naked, by his side.

"Now, that is definitely something I'd travel back in time to experience again." Luciel stated.

"Well, we can if we want." Thrakus replied.

"Shall we?"

"Don't see why not."

"But won't we find ourselves in a causal time loop where we end up shagging infinitely?"

Thrakus grinned "...and what would be wrong with that?"

"Well, nothing except that we're in the middle of a bloody war here."

Thrakus sighed "War. Always a cock blocker."

"Of course, the war did not interrupt our session, did it?"

Thrakus perked up. "Indeed not."

...and thus, they went back in time again...and again...and again...

--

That night, Rodney had many dreams. His subconscious was reflecting on the fact that he had been through a lot over the past few days. His subconscious considered that now, finally, he was free of his boring life. Yes, there was a war going on, and his subconscious, as well as his conscious, had no idea how big this war was or what was at stake exactly, but that was mysterious – it had some intrigue, and that definitely was not boring. His subconscious was reflecting how much Rodney had grown as a person over the past few days. He found himself in a dark room with a spotlight on a gorilla. The gorilla wore a party hat and held a red balloon in its right hand. It beckoned Rodney to come hither and bore an expression that doctors who have ever given bad news to a patient's family would be intimately familiar with. Rodney walked up to the gorilla. Rodney knelt down and the gorilla spoke into his ear.

"Fear not, Rodney, for I am Kinky the psychic gorilla."

"Bu...wha--" was all he could muster.

"...I already know what you're going to say."

"Even--"

"'This'? Yes."

Rodney backed away. "So, what are you doing here?"

"I'm here to warn you about your friend Marwood."

"What about him?"

"He needs to die."

"Needs to...what?!" Rodney suddenly realized he was exclaiming at his subconscious.

"He needs to die. The universe -- indeed all of space -- can only be safe without Marwood around."

Rodney stayed silent. His subconscious was playing tricks. Good tricks, though, he thought.

"There is a dark day ahead. There is one other who knows of this, but he has been trapped due to his own carelessness..."

"This is my subconscious. You don't exist."

"You're right about that first one -- this is your subconscious." Kinky smiled, and a lever appeared. Kinky pulled it.

A door on the far left of the room opened and light emitted from it. A woman exited from it. She was relatively short and in good shape. She had dark brown short hair and blue eyes. She was wearing blue faded jeans, a black t-shirt and a denim jacket. She turned and saw Rodney.

"Rodney!" She exclaimed.

Rodney's jaw dropped. "...Tina?! What are you doing here?"

Tina looked towards the floor. "I don't know. One moment I was just walking around town, the next I was in this...dungeon. I was held captive by this...gorilla. It gave me the most intimidating stare, wagging its finger at me, and occasionally throwing squares of chocolate in my direction." She paused, lifted her head, made eye contact and a small smile formed across her face. "Oh Rodney, I'm so glad you're here." She did, however, make no attempt for physical contact. Her eyes glared back at the floor. "I know we didn't leave it on the best of terms..."

"You called security on me."

"You were drunk and being aggressive."

"You were feeling up some other guy."

"...but I always said I was going home with you."

"Still, no excuse." Rodney replied. They both sighed.

"Look, that was in the past--" Rodney started just as Kinky stood up and charged towards him. The gorilla got right up in his face.

"Don't you dare!" Kinky exclaimed.

"What?" Rodney replied.

Kinky snapped her fingers and Tina disappeared in a puff of smoke. "All I was trying to do was show you that this place was indeed your subconscious."

"Then what harm would --"

"It's part of my psychic link. I can manifest the imaginary and make it real--"

"Again, what harm would it do? It has been a while since I've gotten any..."

"The Universe is in enough trouble without you

getting it on with the bitch from Hell. The woman is evil Rodney. True evil, and you know this."

"You mean she's part of this war?"

Kinky backed away and laughed heartily. "Oh Rodney -- that was good. An absolute classic." Kinky rolled on the ground laughing and giggling. "She would put the enemy out of commission just by seducing them." Kinky laughed a bit more, then got up and attempted to compose herself. "She's no more of a part of the war than any other ordinary human being -- but she is a cheating slut."

"Actually, she never --"

"Silence Rodney. I'm not your therapist."

All of a sudden, the scenery started to change. Everything about the scenery took a blocky shape, as if from a late 80's video game. The walls went from black (or at least perceived to be black) to dark red and the ceiling flipped over, now possessing a chandelier. The room was now well lit, and in the middle, there was a coffee table with a chessboard set up and ready to play.

"Have a seat." Kinky instructed.

They both took a seat at the table.

"What are we still doing here?"

"Even though this contains elements of your subconscious, it is not a dream. I am about to prove this to you."

"How?"

"Well when you're in a dream and you know it, you can control things just by thinking about them. So, move a pawn with your mind."

Rodney concentrated hard for a moment on moving e2 to e4, and then a thought occurred. "So, if I can move the pawn, you'll fuck off, right?"

"Right, and if you can't move it, I'll still fuck off –

you've heard all that you need to."

The pawn remained still for all eternity.

CHAPTER 8

TRIPPIN' DOWN MEMORY LANE

It was dark when he arose. In. Out. Breathing seemed normal. But it was pitch black. He patted himself down. Jeans, wallet, keys were there. Feeling further up, he found he was wearing a velvet jacket. But there was something amiss.

Suddenly, there was a brief light, and a cloud of smoke materialized.

"Welcome back, Mr. Locosa." The voice boomed.

"Yo, fam. Gimme my phone back!"

The voice boomed a chuckle. "Oh Nigel. Where you're going, you're not...going to need a phone."

There was a snapping of fingers to reveal lights on the wall. The lights revealed the ground to be damp. The pitter-patter of drops indicated to Nigel that it was currently drizzling. The light also revealed that the finger snapper was someone with horns on their head, purple skinned, dressed in a suit with a silky violet tie, black sports jacket, black slacks, and dark brown loafers. Nigel assumed this person was a man, because the booming voice and the nicely trimmed mustache was evidence against the contrary.

"Who are you?" asked Nigel.

"I am a Demon."

Nigel raised his eyebrows. "A demon?"

"It's Demon, Nigel. Capital D." The Demon replied slowly, almost in pain. "Please, we take that shit very seriously."

"But you don't look like a Demon…?"

"Well, what do you expect a Demon to look like?"

"Well…" Nigel's mind started to wander. He remembered stories of the devil from his time in primary school. Images of brimstone, fire, and a maniac with horns with a three-pronged trident filled his mind. He was not expecting a man with a suit in a pitch black, and rather cold…*hallway?* His brain was still trying to make sense of it all, and there was not enough light to shed on the matter. "…not so…dressed up…" He finally replied.

"In this place, one must look the part." The Demon adjusted his tie "You might have noticed your clothes have changed slightly."

Nigel looked down at himself and sported a quizzical eye. "Why?"

"As I said, to look the part. Come with me"

The men started walking down what seemed to be a narrow alley. Nigels noticed that every part of the pavement he stepped on glowed momentarily until he released his foot.

"Where are we?" Nigel asked.

"Welcome to the Spiritual Realm, Mr. Locosa."

"Why is it glowing on the ground?"

The Demon looked down at Nigel's feet, slightly bemused. He gave no answer.

Nigel waited a beat. "And why me?"

The Demon raised his eyebrow slightly. "Why not you? After all, you did help me out…"

Nigel stopped; confusion started to reign across his

face. "Eh?"

"I motorcycled my way through France, and you gave me directions."

Nigel thought for a moment. "France. Wow. That seems so long ago now."

"Yes, well," The Demon produced a cane and went onwards. "Time does weird things up here."

Nigel rolled his eyes. "Where are we going?"

The Demon stopped and looked at him. *Now is a good time.* He thought. and he struck the end of the cane to the ground with a hard thud, causing the ground he struck to glow in the exact same way as Nigel's footsteps. "This cane..."

Nigel looked at the Demon in disbelief. "No fucking way am I going inside that cane!"

"No, no. You see, this cane has a lot of power here. Blessed by an ethereal being of high ranking; hence the glow."

"Uh huh..."

The bemused look returned upon the Demon's face. "When you walk, Nigel Locosa, the glow happens naturally. We need to find out why."

Onwards they walked until they got to the end of the alley. At the end of the alley was the Abyss. Or at least that's what Nigel thought.

When Rodney woke up, he found himself in a dark room with a spotlight on in the distance. The spotlight was on Dorius, and Rodney considered how old, yet strong, the man looked. As Dorius approached him. Rodney made no attempt to get up from the bed he was in.

"Welcome to my ship. The Romana XI." Dorius

boomed. "I hope the nightmares didn't frighten you too much."

Rodney remained silent. He pulled his legs towards himself and stood up slowly. Upon completion of this task, it took a further few seconds for him to steady himself.

"People often get weird experiences when they first board this ship." Dorius gave Rodney a friendly pat on the shoulder. "Come now, we have much to discuss."

They strolled out of the room into a hallway. Doors lined the corridor, with numbers on them. Rodney thought this was strange, not because the doors were numbered, but because of the fact that they were numbered with decimals. He passed door 3.2 on his left and 2.27 on his right.

Without missing a beat, Dorius explained: "The doors are numbered this way because we are at arms in this most terrible war. We need sleeping quarters for our numerous soldiers, and the decimal points allow us to save space."

Rodney raised his eyebrows.

"I'll explain once we enter the Planning Deck at the end of this hall." They continued walking until they reached the door at the end of the hall. It was large, green with a gold keypad with what Rodney thought of as "gibberish symbols". Also, there was a keyhole to the right with the phrase "Fuck Off" in red spray paint above it. Dorius sighed.

"Kids....this war has been really harsh on them. Bless." Dorius produced a key that Rodney thought looked odd. It looked like a normal key but was hexagonal at the end. Dorius turned the key, and the door opened.

"Welcome Elder Dorius." The door greeted. "...and

welcome, Companion of the Elder. Can I provide either of you with refreshment?"

"That would be great, door. Thank you." Dorius replied.

"It is my pleasure. Ether-tea ok for both of you?"

"Ether-tea sounds grand for the both of us!"

"What's Ether-tea?" Rodney asked in a hushed tone towards Dorius.

"Ether-tea combines the nourishment of tea, and the antiseptic effects of alcohol." Dorius paused, as if lost in thought. "But fair warning, it does taste like shit though."

They proceeded down the steps before them. Ahead of them was a central area with a dark blue elliptical glass table which had a distinctive militaristic feel to it and ten chairs surrounding it, equidistant from each other. The men calmly approached the table. Rodney looked around in fascination because it was all new territory to him. The men took seats across from each other at the middle, fat part of the table. As they sat down, two small square sections from the table, measuring about three inches, opened up and propelled up, on each square, a martini glass, and a replacement square. The glass contained steaming greenish-brown liquid and a lemon to garnish.

"Are you sure this isn't just shit?!" Rodney chuckled.

Dorius laughed heartily and raised his glass. "To new war-mates!" Rodney clinked his glass and nodded in acknowledgment. They both sipped their new libations – Rodney spat it out.

"Dear god, it really does taste like shit."

"Get that down ya boy, and you'll be good for three days."

Rodney took another swig and grimaced.

"So, talking door?" Rodney asked.

"Yes. Quite. We used to have servants on this ship, back when I started. But then we ran into financial issues, and the return on investment was higher with subservient doors - they never get the orders wrong, and you don't have to pay them an hourly wage. Plus, we got a hell of a deal..."

"...let me guess, the guy who gave you the deal had two heads?"

"Don't be ridiculous, Rodney! Everybody knows that guy's in a different universe. And anyway, he's far too busy trying to get himself re-elected as galactic president..."

Rodney just stared blankly. "Well, I was just kidding..."

Dorius chuckled. "When you have been in this business for as long as I have, you learn that every possibility exists, somewhere, in some universe...but anyway, down to business. You are from Earth, which is in Real Space --"

"Well, actually, I'm not, apparently. I'm from some other --"

"Yes, yes. Well, that planet too is in Real Space. For now."

"What is Real Space anyway and how does it differ from...Non-Real Space?"

"Real Space is space as you know it. Currently we are not in it. We are in Holographic Space."

"What is this war about anyway?"

"Legend has it, there was this king who wanted an escape from his past. He felt his life was one of dishonor. He fought in a galactic war for his home planet of Califahn and lost. Also lost his parents in the process. He became so distraught by that and the taunting he'd endured from coming out as a homosexual that he just wanted to end it all. That was until one day when he talked to his Vicar, who let him in on a secret about the universe. Soon after this, the captors of his planet left. The man, who was at this point the king of his land, appointed all his royal scientists and researchers to figure out, initially, how to move entire galaxies across to the other side of the universe, so they could all get a new start." Dorius sipped his drink. "Well, it wasn't long until one of the researchers, the head researcher in fact, by the name of Christian Lucifer, figured out how to harness the power from a parallel universe to create an entirely new galaxy--"

Rodney looked slightly puzzled. Dorius picked up on this.

"--OK. So, the king wanted an escape. He wanted an out from his current situation. Christian Lucifer was a brilliant scientist and managed to hack into a parallel universe. A spare one."

"A spare...universe?" Rodney sipped his tea. All parts of him were actually ok with it, except for his taste buds. They would sign a death warrant for him if it meant he could never drink such a vile liquid again.

"Yes. You see, when you have a choice, which creates several parallel universes equaling the number of choices, minus one, to account for the present universe. At least that's one way to create a parallel universe...there are others of course, but we really don't have any time to go into that now..."

"Okay, Isaac Asimov..." Rodney snarked. Dorius chose to ignore it.

"So anyway, Christian Lucifer got in contact with a popudei..."

"Thrakus? We met him earlier."

"Well, not him, but one of his kind, yes. This one was grittier. A rogue." Dorius paused. He pressed a button on the desk, which brought up a keyboard and the lights dimmed. Dorius started typing, and something appeared in the center of the desk. It said, "Please enter the gate code."

"You see..." Dorius slowly began. This was complicated, and he was old. So he had to think through this before he said it. "Every universe has a gate code that is needed for entry from another universe."

"Like 1 2 3 4 5 6?" Rodney asked.

"Sure...but a lot more complicated."

"How complicated?"

"Each universe has a descriptor. Usually, it's PU and then a series of letters and numbers after that. There is a lot of talk in this community about what those letters and numbers mean and how they are generated, but for now we assume that they are random.

"Anyway..." Doruis continued. "...the rogue popudei managed to get the descriptor for a universe that would be invoked at some time in the future. About seven Earth years from our current year."

"Because of a choice?"

"We think so, yes. Our evidence does not point towards the more crude ways of creating parallel universes."

"Is it an important choice?"

"God knows."

"Does God exist?"

Dorius sipped his tea and smiled. "Can we please keep on topic?"

Rodney fidgeted. "Yes, of course. So. Descriptor for a universe seven years in the future..."

"Yes, well...this rogue managed to crack the gate-code, but only gave it to Lucifer on one condition. That he-the rogue-would have as much of this new universe as he wanted."

"And he agreed?"

"Lucifer would do anything to show off a bit of tech. Especially if he had something to gain from it. So anyway--" Dorius pressed a button that caused the image to populate a field with eight asterisks and then change the image to what looked like a paper tear among a starry backdrop. A kind of star shaped fracture, with stars inside the area. "--this image isn't necessarily the exact image, but enough to get the point across. Lucifer built a machine that when you put in a gate code for a universe, it can find it, and start projecting from that universe."

"Projecting what?"

"Space. And because of some very tricky dimensional mathematics, he could use very little of this other universe to populate a large area of our own space."

"So, it's like a link to that other universe within ours by means of a holographic projection?" After this, Rodney took a breath, hardly believing what he had just said.

"Yes."

"So, what exists in this new galaxy is actually what exists in that universe?"

"Yes." Dorius paused. "So, Lucifer figured out exactly how much of this universe he'd need to create a galaxy -- and it wasn't much by universe standards -- and he brought up the idea of this holographic galaxy to the king, who thought it was brilliant. Fortune was on their side, as many of the surrounding galaxies on the other side of this universe had blipped out of existence, they had all these spare areas of space that they could use for it – and they did."

"So, what happened?" Rodney paused. He started to think of terms of how this could break out into an actual war. "Obviously Real Space still exists, otherwise Earth, among other places, would be gone, right?"

"That is true, but we don't know how much longer they have…" Dorius paused, took another sip of his Ether-tea and gave a sigh of relaxation. "So. The holographic galaxy was built, and for a good part of what you would consider 50 of your Earth years, things were fine. They had enough room to expand for their every need. But that's not enough for some people…"

Rodney sipped his Ether-Tea, and by this point, his taste buds gave in; It tasted sweet he thought, compared to the bitter taste of war that he was sure was ahead of him. He leaned closer, and Dorius continued.

"He presented an expansion to the galaxy, dubbed 'The Holographic Universe'. The King utterly refused. He refuted it, because he knew the outcome was war, and he didn't want others to suffer as he had suffered. He was right to do so."

"Let me guess. This Christian Lucifer continued anyway? Couldn't they have imprisoned him?"

"Oh, they tried."

"He always got out?"

"He destroyed the prisons." Dorius paused. "He's a very smart being. He had armies on his side. Armies of quantum beings called Maybes."

"Maybes?"

"Yes. Beings that might exist depending on your current state. If you can face them, they are there and exist -- real as anything, but once you turn your back, they blip out of existence. As soon as you turn back again, however, they are still there, pretending never to have moved from your sight."

"Sounds like a pain to defeat."

"Hence why this war became so big – with those things as henchmen."

"But wait, I heard about other races being involved..."

"Quite. Allies with Mr. Lucifer. When they started losing, Lucifer came up with the idea of combining the agility of the Parasites with the cruel intuitiveness of Leatherkind."

To Rodney, this started to sound like gobbledygook, but he ignored it and carried on. "So, what does Christian Lucifer actually want?"

"Well, I think you answered your own question earlier. Christian Lucifer believes Holographic Space is the future...."

"How does this affect this rogue popudei?"

"No idea."

"So, they're expanding it, right?"

"Well, sure." Dorius sighed. "But the main issue behind it all is that he needs to make room for it -- the entire universe as we know it-- destroying everything in the process."

"Why can't we just join it? You said we were in Holographic Space right now..."

"We're incognito."

Of course we are, Rodney thought. "Still..."

"Because from his point of view, we are of the Old Universe, and must be discarded."

"How do you get all this information anyway?"

"We have our sources. Mostly spies from within the

King's palace. For a long time, we knew something would happen when he came to power. So we put in spies as insurance. As it happens, that worked out. We'd be sitting ducks otherwise."

"...and what makes you so sure you're not sitting ducks now?"

Silence fell upon the table and passed out. It was at this point that Rodney was reminded of what Kinky had said to him. Is Marwood truly the legitimate threat here? Even if he was, surely it couldn't compare to the threat that Christian Lucifer and this rogue popudei presented, right?...and then it all came flooding back.

Marwood drove along a lonely road in his newly reconstructed van.

"Thank God everything can be reconstructed in Holographic Space..." He muttered to himself. Then...

"Oh fuck!" Marwood exclaimed.

In the middle of the street, he rapidly applied the brakes as Kinky the Psychic Gorilla suddenly appeared right in front of him. He got out of the car and looked around – nothing in sight.

"Ooooh, fuck." Marwood brooded to himself. He stepped away from the car about ten paces.

From behind him, a soft female voice emanated. "Hello, Marwood."

"Hey Kinky..." Marwood replied, rather shakily.

Kinky moved in front of Marwood. "You know, there's no need to be nervous around me. After all, you did free me."

"What do you want, Kinky?"

"What does any normal girl want?"

"Love? Romance?"

"Banana."

"Banana…what?"

"The philosophy of Banana. Once you find banana, you are one with the universe…"

"So, what you are looking for is peace?"

"…in this war it isn't so easy to find."

"The war is tough, Kinky, but peace is individual. You can find peace anywhere if you make room for it."

"Well, we have two popudeis trapped in a hedonistic cycle…"

"What?"

"Oh …ummm…nothing…" Kinky bit her bottom lip. Marwood suddenly felt unable to speak for a few moments, at which point, awkwardness took stage right.

"…are you trying to seduce me?" Marwood innocently inquired.

"Me? No, of course not."

"Then why are you here?"

"I'm here to give you a chance."

"A chance? A chance for what?"

Kinky looked up and down the street and saw that it was clear. "Come on, Marwood. Walk with me." Kinky offered her hand upwards to him. He ignored it.

"No, of course not." She muttered to herself, and they walked.

Nigel and his Demon companion stopped in the darkness. The Demon snapped his fingers, and a flame appeared in his hand. The flame revealed faint green portals on the far sides around them.

"We're here." The Demon said.

"What are those green portals on the walls?"

"These are not walls, Nigel. At least not the kinds of

which you're accustomed to."

"...and the portals?"

"Those are gateways to Ultra Space."

"What's Ultra Space?" Nigel asked.

"Ultra Space is a hedonistic galactic sector in a parallel universe. We have hired monks from there."

"Parallel universe?! What the fuck are they doing here?"

"Helping us fight in the war. They guard the underworlds."

"Wait, I thought we had other guardians of the underworld..."

The Demon laughed lightly. "Those people are lying..."

"So what makes these monks so important?"

"Well, they deal with the most hedonistic people and environments in their universe, and they don't even get tempted -- their willpower and sense of commitment is that strong, so when they are called to defend an underworld, they really fucking defend it."

"I'd hate to see the bill for them at the end of all this."

The Demon grinned. "They're independent contractors too. They get to write off travel expenses."

"From another universe? Blimey."

"Quite. But in the name of peace, the pockets go deep."

Nigel nodded. In the distance, chanting could be heard. The Demon placed a hand on Nigel's shoulder.

"Welcome to the Domain of the Ultra Space Monks." The Demon said, then removed his arm. "But this is not our destination."

"Where are we going?"

"Mr. Locosa, we are going to the Soul Realm."

Nigel's head was still spinning from the Monks of

Ultra Space. *Soul realm??*

"Sssssh..." The Demon ushered.

Nigel switched his attention straight to the Demon, who felt he himself was being interrupted. "No, I can't hear your thoughts exactly, but I can see the outline of them...." He paused for a second, and looked at the ground, which your average being couldn't quite make out. To Nigel, it was black as charcoal. To the Demon, however, the ground was beautiful; he could see all the colors of the spectrum in shapes that humans had yet to have names for, but he knew what this place was, what it represented, and he knew he better not do wrong by it. "Listen, I apologize for not being straight with you earlier. I just had to....gauge your meter. Make sure you are up to snuff."

"....and?"

The Demon smiled. "You're still here, aren't you?" He snapped his fingers.

Lights appeared. Light jazz music started playing in the background, and appearing in front of the men was a table with two chairs and two places set. The Demon ushered Nigel towards it.

"What? Are we on a date?" Nigel asked cheekily.

"Well..." The Demon replied. "You are wearing a rather dashing velvet jacket..."

Kinky and Marwood walked down a barren street. The houses on either side were crumbling. There were kids running around and playing. There was a group playing dodgeball with a bowling ball (the ball had been configured to be light in terms of weight and damage potential, so it was considered "safe" under the Galactic Act for Safer Toys). The boy throwing the ball turned around and saw Marwood and Kinky, dropped the ball (which due to its gravitational value, just sat in mid-air) and shouted back to his boys.

"Squaddies, we have a gorilla!" The group began to swarm towards them.

"Aww, I just want to cuddle him!" exclaimed a random boy.

Kinky and Marwood looked at each other with widened eyes, turned around and started running back up the street. They went over a hill, jumped a couple of fences, and found a small hookah shop, in which they entered and locked the door behind them. Marwood started fiddling with his watch, and the door glowed green. They slumped over, trying to get their breath back. Once standing again normally, they looked around. The shop was a small wooden hut, with some oriental looking wall scrolls, and a middle-aged bald man in army gear behind the counter was smoking a pipe and reading the paper. They approached him slowly, with caution.

"Bloody kids. Glad you locked the door." The man said softly whilst turning the page in his paper. He looked up, and locked eyes with Marwood. He puffed and removed his pipe from his mouth. Marwood's eyes widened.

"You don't have to worry, you know. I'm not of this universe..." The man began.

"Then how...?" Marwood asked.

"Same way you people did. But come, now, I believe they said you needed a hookah..." The man beckoned Marwood and Kinky to come into the back area with him, but the two stood still.

"They? Who are they?" Marwood inquired.

Kinky whispered very softly in Marwood's ear. "We are expected, does it really matter who by?"

Marwood leaned against a nearby chair and twitched for a moment. He took off his glasses and wiped the sweat from his brow. For a moment, he thought it was just generally hot, but then he caught a glimpse of the thermostat on the wall . It was set to 55 degrees Fahrenheit. It was him. Just him. And his temperature was rising.

"Well, yes, of course it does! We're in the middle of a war, Kinky! If I'm expected somewhere mysteriously, it might be a trap!" Marwood breathed a sigh of relief, and then his temperature plummeted back to normal. War was stressful, taking its toll on anyone of either side, regardless of their level of involvement. Sometimes just getting your words out can be considered a victory.

Kinky knelt down to Marwood, in front of the chair, and put her arm on his shoulder.

"Alright, you big bloody brilliant man, you got me. I knew we were expected. I..." Kinky looked down towards the ground. "...I'm sorry I didn't tell you earlier."

Marwood looked directly into Kinky's eyes. His great blue-green eyes stared into the very depths of her soul.

"Kinky..."

"Yes, Marwood?"

"Why are we expected?"

"Because we need to talk."

"About what?"

"About you."

"Why me?"

"Come on, let's go into the back area, we can discuss it all there."

"..." Marwood got up from the chair, and together, they both approached the man.

"We have a very special blend, just for you. It's called

The Ethereal." The three entered the back area.

The back area was low-lit, with the same Asian scrolls as the front. A disco ball hung from the center of the room, and the sound of light dubstep played from a small stereo in the far-left corner of the room. Sofas lined most of the room's edge near a long plank of wood, acting as a very long table, beginning where the line of couches began and ended in a similar fashion. Sofas also lined up on the other side of the wood, again in a similar fashion. Quietly, Marwood and Kinky slipped into the end where the sofas began. They had, however, no reason to be quiet, as there were no other souls around--save for themselves, the bald man, and the safety inspector, who was working on some pipes in the bathroom down the hall.

"Jack! We have a bit of a situation here!" A voice screamed from the bathroom. To Marwood, the voice sounded familiar.

The bald man answered. "What? Can I at least give these guys their hookah?" He loaded up a hookah, put it down at the table near Marwood and Kinky, and walked into the bathroom. "Well, sure, but absolutely no one must go into that bathroom until this damned toilet gets fixed!" Boomed the safety inspector.

"Oh, Mike..."

Mike looked at Jack. Their eyes met, and Mike was staring hard, then reached into his pocket and produced a gun. He pointed it right at Jack's face. Jack raised his hands.

"Jack, now, tell me, who took a shit so massive in the toilet that it broke."

Jack stared at the metallic tube, mere millimeters from his nose, yet remained totally calm. After all, he had been through worse. In a very soft voice, he mentioned,

"You know who."

Mike raised his head a little, looking down at Jack and gave a big sniff. "The Shitmeister!" Mike lowered his gun slowly and put it away. Jack lowered his hands and produced a small red tin. "I think it's time for a safety meeting. What do you say?" Mike gestured for Jack to open the tin. He did so, and Mike grinned, because inside was a bag of some of the best dank this side of the Universe. The men walked through the main room, completely ignoring the guests and exited through the front. Marwood managed to catch a glimpse of Mike's fingers, the nail portions of which were decorated in the color of daffodils. He noted that this was slightly out of the ordinary and thought nothing else of the matter.

"Well..." Kinky started as both her and Marwood turned away from staring at the men and turned their attention to each other. "...that was unexpected." Kinky started puffing the hookah. "Hoo wee! That's some good shit!" At this point, the stereo started blasting some reggae. "Now then, down to business..."

Rodney slumped his head on the table and groaned. Images flashed through his head: lying in a cot in a small economy-sized spaceship, the Class-M Space Jockey. It had enough to seat three, with some storage compartments at the back. His mother looked down at him, her face with a backdrop of the many stars behind her.

"You'll get to see them all." She said.

Rodney gurgled happily.

"You'll make us proud, son. You'll get to be a hero and live amongst those stars."

Above his cot, there was a mobile of stars and planets. Rodney started to bat at them.

"There's my boy. Now..." His mother's voice dropped into a much softer and whispered tone. "...we won't get to see you again, for a very long time. But one day, we will meet again. And when you remember this, it's a sign that it won't be too long."

With that, his mother kissed him on the forehead and turned back to the cockpit, and eventually they landed on a planet. His mother picked him up from the cot and, with her husband accompanying her, delivered him to a man, and then went back into their spaceship, which gave off a bright white light and disappeared. The man she gave Rodney to was slightly tall and of a bulky build. He was dressed in a white coat and had a thick black beard. The first thing that Rodney noted about him was that it was night...and the man was wearing sunglasses.

He started to stir awake and tried to compose himself in front of the elder, with whom he was previously conversing with.

"Yeah, the ether-tea will do that to you..." Dorius remarked.

Rodney lifted his head ever so slightly and looked at Dorius straight in the eye. "I remember now."

"Well, good. Can you tell me what it is that you remember?"

"My parents..."

"They sacrificed a lot for you."

"But why can I remember? Aren't we supposed to have infantile amnesia? At least that's what I learned in school..."

"Human school perhaps. That condition does not affect true Somerfieldians."

"Where did they go? Their ship just sort of....disappeared."

"I don't know. But I have faith..." Dorius paused "...that you will know where and why someday soon."

Marwood took a puff of the hookah. He smoke-dragoned through his nose. From Kinky's point of view, his head was obstructed by smoke for a few seconds. As his face silhouetted into view, he asked "So why are we here?"

"My dear Marwood. There are many of us in the psychic community."

"I know."

"...and we can foretell the end, and that you are the one responsible for it."

"The end of what?"

"The end of everything."

Marwood took a deeper puff of the hookah. He puffed it out and relaxed on the couch. "But you and I both know that foretelling the end of everything does not indeed mean the literal end of all things. After all, death in a Tarot reading signifies mere change."

"You have a good point...one that we in the psychic community have considered. But we must be realistic."

"Realistic?"

"Look at this place. The only reason why we're still alive here is because this very building is imported from, technically, another universe."

"I know...and if those kids actually made physical contact with us, we would have died instantly."

"Exactly."

"So, what you're saying is that the end must come?"

"I cannot say either way. But there will be others in the community who may be after you." At this point, she took his hand into her lap, and squeezed. "I know

what mission lies ahead for you, and thus I must bid you
Godspeed, Marwood--May you lead us all to a better place
than this."

CHAPTER 9

DEEPER DOWN THE RABBIT HOLE

Nigel and the Demon sat down at the table. Nigel looked around. Not a portal in sight.

"Where did the portals go?" He asked.

"Oh, they're still there." The Demon replied. "But, for now, it's not important for us to see them, so we can't."

"But they're still there, right?"

The Demon nodded happily.

"We can go through them still, right?"

The Demon's expression dropped. "It's one way. If you tried, you'd get scattered across the cosmos, so I wouldn't if I were you."

"I see."

"So…" The Demon started. Goblets of red wine materialized before them. "Let's talk about your death."

Nigel took a big swig of wine. Courage found him once again. "What about it?"

"What did you experience?" The Demon asked, slowly sipping his wine.

"It was instantaneous." Nigel took another gulp.

"It was said that you died with a smile upon your face, though when I reached you, you had no such expression…?"

"Well…" Nigel thought very carefully about how to

put it. "I had stuff to say, but in the end, you can't beat the finality of death."

"Quite" The Demon paused. "...that is quite in contrast to your earlier...more carefree self."

Nigel finished his wine and smashed the goblet against the table. "I guess death really changes a person."

The Demon smiled. "I think you're ready."

"For what?"

The Demon rose from his chair. "Follow me."

Nigel walked with the Demon out of their little dining area until they reached a flight of stairs, then they ascended. As they ascended, the light slowly diminished. When they reached the top, below them was darkness. They found that they were in a narrow hallway with a platform in the middle, and a group of monks walking back and forth, chanting in, as far as Nigel was concerned, complete gibberish.

"What are they chanting?" Nigel asked.

"The Protection Prayer." The Demon replied.

"Does that honestly work?"

"Well, we're not dead right now, are we?"

Nigel thought. "Wait a second...I thought we were in the Spiritual Realm..."

"Yes", The Demon started. "We are. The monks enter through here, and they will protect us all the way through the Underworld."

"Why am I here?" Nigel asked.

"In case they fail. Think of yourself as an insurance policy."

At this point, the entirety of the Spiritual Realm shook like nothing else. One of the monks was on the platform and announced "We may be under attack soon. Prepare yourself with the power of prayer!" The monks started chanting faster, and occasionally would raise up their palms which after a second, a glowing blue energy ball would appear. The palms would then thrust forward, and the balls would then move to the ceiling, causing it to glow blue. The monks practiced this behavior in times of need but there were a few who were skeptical as to whether it worked. It actually did, so they were correct in thinking this, but only because the vast majority believed it to be so. On a nearby wall, a blue portal appeared.

"This is our stop." The Demon said, gesturing towards the portal. "Come on; let's go!" And with that, both beings entered.

Thrakus was about to harness some technology. Not the kind of technology Christian Lucifer harnesses, however. What Thrakus was about to harness was technology from a very particular parallel universe -- one kept well secret in certain circles, for if the information got into the wrong hands, it would be the multiversal equivalent of nuclear warfare.

In his downtime between dropping the guys off at the Underworld and meeting Luciel for a paradoxical experience he would never forget, he went to Jeff and Ben's office.

"Thrakus. Good to see you!" Jeff exclaimed.

"Hey Jeff, I need to use your projection servers real quick." Thrakus swiftly replied.

"Why?"

"Look at your server logs for Earth."

Ben turned and chimed in with a concerned look upon his face. "He's right. We should just do what he says."

The projection servers for a planet allows someone

to send a hologram of themselves to anywhere on the planet. Usually, they're just pre-programmed subroutines for leaving messages. Primitive projection servers had been around for years in the Underworld; that's why ghosts exist. Jeff brought Thrakus over to a large shiny black server tower. Attached was an IV.

"Now, I'm going to put this in your arm." Jeff mentioned. Thrakus nodded. Jeff inserted the IV. Thrakus twitched violently for a second. The touchscreen monitor attached asked Thrakus a few questions, mostly asking for his permission regarding the installed security protocols, which he answered in the affirmative.

"*Downloading image...*" The machine boomed in a very demanding voice.

Everyone was tense for just a few seconds.

"*Downloaded image. You can now safely disconnect. Jeff, could I please have a cup of tea?!?!*" The machine boomed again.

Jeff sighed. "No, you can't. You're a fucking machine! Now act like one!" He disconnected Thrakus. "Sorry about that. The manufacturer resided in a parallel universe and thought it'd be funny to give personalities to machines."

"Then why didn't you go with another manufacturer?"

Jeff sighed again. "There is no other manufacturer for these higher end machines."

"Huh. I see."

"What time would you like this projection to go out?"

Thrakus looked at his watch. "In about five hours will do."

"Did you select the spontaneous intelligence option?"

"Of course." Spontaneous Intelligence is only done

with the express permission of the subject, as it hides nothing. It has to use the entire brain in order to make decisions just as the subject would in any given situation instead of forty percent that it would otherwise do, allowing it to be a clone of sorts. Following this, Thrakus zoomed out of the building for a timeless encounter with a fellow popudei.

Caroline was curled up in a ball by the sofa in her living room when the doorbell rang. Shakily, she rose from the floor, clenching a Red Nose Day-themed stress ball in her left hand. When she opened the door, a man with spiky black hair (almost like his head was full of mohawks),wearing a leather jacket appeared on the other side.

"Caroline Holmes?" Thrakus addressed her. Caroline's eyes widened.

"Get away from me..." She croaked. From her pocket, she produced a steak knife and held it against Thrakus' chin. He raised his arms. "...no man shall enter this house, and that includes you!" Caroline hissed, putting her hand on the door in preparation for closing it.

"Well, actually, ma'am, I'm not here to enter your house..." He wiggled his hands and lowered them slowly. She retracted the knife and loosened her grip on the door. Thrakus breathed a sigh of relief.

Caroline spoke rather agitatedly. "Well, if you can do it from the doorstep, what are you here for?"

"I'm here to give you a message."

"Who from?"

"From me."

"Okay..."

Thrakus looked at his feet. "Your brother is doing

well."

Water started to form around her eyes. A single tear dripped down her face in a rather casual manner. Then, another, and another. After a few seconds, the floodgates opened. Slowly, she slumped over. Thrakus approached her just as slowly and wrapped his arms around her. Softly, she wept into his chest.

"I can't believe I forgot about my own brother!" She exclaimed.

"Well, it's hardly surprising. I mean, they did take your soul away."

She raised her head and looked at him. The soulless know a real person when they see one. As soon as she mentally noted his appearance, the first thing that came to her mind was "...and you're talking to me about being soulless?!" She started weeping stronger, but only part of that was due to feeling some self-pity knowing that she was being comforted by some strange being.

"Why did they do that?" Caroline asked.

"Now, Caroline." Thrakus said. "You're going to have to be very strong for this next part." She looked up at him again.

"Now, look into my eyes. It's okay, you're safe. You have no soul." Eye contact was immediately established, and almost immediately afterwards, her eyes dried.

"Good. Now, let's go for a walk." Thrakus suggested.

Marwood and Kinky both walked out of the hookah bar. Mike and Jack were still smoking up a storm. Jack had the pipe and passed it to Kinky. She touched the bowl and it lit. One notable thing about psychic creatures is that they have no need for lighters if they were smoking. Strangely enough, it took the psychic community a long time to discover this, as most psychics saw a bad future for themselves if they partook. Later on, however, it was discovered that their psychic vision was ironically clouded due to the lack of smoking. Kinky took a puff.

"Neat trick you got there." Jack started. Kinky smiled mischievously.

"So, what were y'all talking about in there?" Mike asked.

"Well, um...stuff." Marwood replied, remembering his last encounter with the man, and wanting to remain intentionally vague. "Complicated, wacko space type...stuff."

"I'd answer him straight if I were you." Jack suggested.

"Yes, I would too." Mike chimed in as he grabbed his gun and pointed it to Marwood's head. "...otherwise, this time, I'll make sure you forget everything...." A grin crept across his face. "...permanently."

"Oh jeez..." Marwood muttered under his breath. He started fiddling with his watch.

"...and don't think your fancy time field stuff will work here either! This very place is imported data from the Old Universe. It is a fact in the New Universe. You cannot do anything to it. It is encrypted."

Marwood hastily pointed towards the building. "But it worked in there."

"Indoor structures can retain their Old Universe properties. It is only the area on which it stands that needs to be imported and encrypted."

"...and you did all this?"

"Yes, I did. And hence I say with confidence..." Mike started grinding his teeth. "...your petty little time fields will not work out here." Mike lowered his voice, "Now, will you please tell us what y'all were talking about in there? It is a matter of Universal security."

Kinky sighed, for she knew what must happen next. She held her hands up slightly and walked in front of Marwood. "Now, Mister Danger, you're better than this."

"How did you..." Mike and Kinky locked eyes. He had no choice but to stare and momentarily lose himself. Her eyes pulled him in. He knew a psychic by the way that they can pull beings into their heads. And he knew what must happen next, given the current state of this universe. "...Oh, no, no no. Not this. Not now." He lowered his head and put both of his hands on his face.

"Then you must know what you need to do."

He raised his head above his hands and looked straight into her eyes. A single tear crept down his face.

With Marwood, he was just playing, but Mike actually hated killing strangers, for the simple fact that he did not know anything of their past. If he did not know their past, then he had absolutely no inkling of what their future might contain. Now, people change, and Mike knew that, but even still, the act of killing someone is a very intimate moment. You get to hear their last words, their dying screams, their final moments on this plane of existence, which could include twitches, mini-seizures, inconsistent breaths, or some combination thereof. This is not something a stranger should be privy to, because they lack the context with which to put all of this in, and that's just being rude. Mike hated being rude for rudeness' sake, however, psychics such as Kinky in the new universe acted like a GPS signal for the Maybes. Once they latched on Kinky, they all would die, and all old-universe properties with them. He couldn't take that risk, but at the same time, doing the right thing was far from easy.

"I can't!" He whimpered.

"You must."

He raised his arm slowly, trembling, and pointed his gun at her. Kinky closed her eyes. He pulled the trigger.

Click. The barrel was empty, and thus no shot was fired. Kinky opened one eye, to be sure, and then she opened another, ever so slightly relieved.

"I think it's best if y'all scram outta here, don't you?" Mike suggested.

"Yes. Come on Marwood. Let's go." They ran back to the van in a rather hasty manner. They threw the doors open, again rather hastily, and slammed them shut behind them in the same manner.

"What was that all about?"

"Marwood - just drive!"

"Where to?"

"Your ship might be a good start."...and thus, they drove. At a particular point, wings protruded from the van, and they flew up into the sky to meet the ship. They docked. They opened the doors, and above them a male computerized voice bellowed at them.

"Welcome home, Marwood Somerfield, and welcome Kinkiforous the Forth of the Psychic Realm."

"Yes, thank you, Prototype." Marwood replied. He sighed. The computer was all around the docking station, which resembled a 21st century gas station. On top housed the central hub which resembled a green glowing version of a big bulky mainframe from the 1970s. "The computer was called Prototype because that's what it was. Having a computer with psychic abilities was considered pretty cool about 25 years prior to this particular point in time, so we decided to build one. We're still working out some of the kinks."

"Ooh!" Kinky exclaimed excitedly. "What kinks?"

"Watch this." Out of his pocket, Marwood produced a bottle of Jack Daniels. He held it high, well within the range of Prototype's sensors. "Prototype, identify material?"

"Sure Marwood. What material would you like me to identify?"

"The material I'm holding up."

"But you're not holding anything up!"

Marwood turned to Kinky. "See? Doesn't work on alcohol."

"Actually, you're wrong."

"...and how do you know that?"

Kinky looked at Marwood and grinned. "...because I'm psychic."

Kinky suddenly produced a bottle of clear liquid.

Marwood raised his eyebrows quizzically. "Where did you get that from?"

Kinky locked her deep black eyes with the highly mysterious forms that represented Marwood's eyes. A warm smile spread across her face. "Trust me, you don't want to know..."

Kinky raised the bottle high, so the computer could sense it.

"Prototype, identify material?"

"Sure Kinkiforous. The material is Everclear."

She turned back to Marwood and smiled innocently.

"It only doesn't work on dark alcohols." She replied.

Marwood stepped forward with a slightly aggressive yet playful glimmer in his eyes. "Cheater! You cheated."

"Nu-uh! You're such a sore loser, but then again, you are a man. You probably just need to get laid!"

Marwood stared daggers into Kinky's eyes, and they

both froze. Slowly, she looked off to the side slightly, like she was processing some information. "...but not now. There's a war going on..."

--

The road was long, but Thrakus and Caroline still embarked upon their voyage through the tiny town in which she lived. Eventually shops appeared.

"What's it like?" Thrakus asked.

"What's what like?"

"Having no soul..."

"Well, everything is in black, white and various shades of grey..."

"Colorless. Interesting..."

They walked by a wine shop on the right-hand side. Thrakus motioned towards it.

"Shall we?"

"Doesn't make any difference to me. Everything just tastes as grey now." Caroline said stoically. Thrakus stopped for a moment and thought.

"Why?"

"No soul, remember?"

"No, I mean Why. You have limited vision, limited taste..."

"...why don't I just give up?" Caroline laughed hysterically for a second before returning to her emotionless self. "I've often asked myself the same thing."

"It's good."

"Good? Good how?" Caroline was starting to get frustrated with where this conversation was going.

"Good that you didn't...you know... kill yourself."

"I couldn't quite bring myself to it. There was this one time. I went to B&Q to buy a chainsaw. I got home and took it out of the box and went out with it into the back garden. When I stepped out, I saw a squirrel eating a nut on the patio. So, content with itself. It had found what it wanted. It had purpose and meaning in its life. So, I turned on the chainsaw and shoved it through the hairy little bugger. At first there was a high-pitched screech --"

At this point, Thrakus put his left hand over his mouth, almost feeling the need to throw up. He stopped himself though.

"I was hoping that by doing this, I'd find the same meaning. But there was none. All there was, was blood. So much blood. Blood I had to clean up. At that point, I decided I simply didn't want to burden anyone with such a thing..."

"...you know, you could have hanged yourself or something."

"Still...having to deal with a corpse, a dead body...that someone else would have to clean up..."

"Good point." Thrakus paused. "Glad you're thinking of others."

Nigel and the Demon appeared in what looked like a barren landscape with lots of stars in the sky.

"Oh shit." The Demon remarked.

Nigel looked around. "What? What's the matter?"

The Demon gestured upwards "Look at the sky."

Nigel looked up. He didn't see anything out of the ordinary. The Demon sighed... "...of course..." he muttered to himself. He took a deep breath. "There are meant to be souls traveling...'in the sky' here."

Nigel interjected. "You hesitated about 'in the sky'...?"

"Well, it's not really the sky. It's the cosmos. Up here, there is no atmosphere."

"Then how are we breathing?"

The Demon looked at Nigel dumbfounded. "Well, I'm a Demon. I'm what you would call undead. I would have to be destroyed in my entirety to not exist anymore. As in all my atoms separated. And you..."

Nigel perked up his full attention. "...you died in the Underworld."

"But...all the stuff in the Spiritual Realm...."

"Still dead. You are only here in spirit, Mister Locosa. No respiratory system. No need for breathing."

Nigel patted himself down. Almost metallic. No flesh to speak of.

"...and the metal. Is that normal?"

"For certain individuals, yes."

Nigel figured asking further might just confuse his brain right now. His expression dropped. Yes, the finality of death hit him after Christian Lucifer's interference with his flesh, but he thought that maybe whatever deity that exists out there gave him a second chance with his voyage with the Demon. He however thought it best not to bring it up now. But the Demon saw the outline of this thought process.

"Tough break, kid. Look, here's a snifter." From his jacket, the Demon produced two glasses of very fine liquor.

Nigel took a sip. "Scotch?"

"Only the best." The Demon remarked. "Fun fact: did you know some of the best scotch makers are dead? We really do get the best scotches up here..."

"Wait...but without organs ...where does it go?"

"Oh...." The Demon started. "...it makes you feel good and then just goes into the air."

"Pffft..." Nigel suspected that this was bullshit.

"No, it's true." The Demon replied. "Getting drunk

with none of the aftereffects. This is the reason why so many people commit suicide."

Nigel's jaw gave way to gravity. "Now, there's no time for that." The Demon explained. "We have people to meet and things to do." Nigel shook off the shock. They both took swigs of the scotch from their glasses. The Demon finished first. As he took his last sip, the glass started dematerializing into the surrounding air. He gestured towards it.

"Pretty neat, eh?"

Nigel just raised his eyebrows and finished. He didn't seem phased by the dematerialization.

The Demon looked closer upon his friend.

"Ah." The Demon surmised. "I've been rambling too much. Well, to be expected, I suppose. There was a lot to explain."

"But you haven't explained anything relevant." Nigel replied.

"Big picture, Mister Locosa. The souls may be out, but the stars are still there."

"Meaning what?"

"Meaning ...we need you to meet some fellow spirits to help in the fight for this great Universe."

"Universe?"

"Well, this part of it. We can't defend the entire Universe. That would be impossible...."

"So..." Nigel shuffled his hands in anticipation. It was the first time he felt his own hands...they looked normal, but they felt so hard and metallic. "...who are we meeting first?"

"An associate of mine called Elkridge. We can reach him on the Far Planes, about 3 miles west of here."

"Another spiritual being?"

"Quite." The Demon gave a look of quiet dread, for he knew what was ahead. "Thankfully, in the Spiritual Realm, we can travel quite fast."

"Right..."

They moved west about three miles. The experience from Nigel's point of view felt like being shoved into a tube and having the force of gravity just letting you fall to your destination. This, in fact, was not far from the truth. The way traveling in the Spiritual Realm works is due to low levels of psychic energy in the air. The destination is always known, so the Realm spawns a travel tube, inside of which can pull the passenger with a velocity of 53 m/s which just so happens to be the terminal velocity of a falling human on Earth, so from a human's point of view (or rather a human's spirit point of view), this means of travel is extremely fast. When they stopped, Nigel felt the need to throw up, but due to his currently ethereal nature, lacked the necessary apparatus to do so.

In the distance, they saw someone who looked like an old monk, and approached him.

"Stay here." The Demon instructed. He went on ahead and whispered something in Elkridge's ear. Elkridge was dressed in traditional monk robes and had a long brown-grey-white beard. He carefully approached Nigel, nodded and smiled.

"My son..." he started. He took Nigel's left hand and enclosed his hands around it. The enclosure glowed green. He let go.

"What the fuck was that shit?!" Nigel politely inquired. He staggered back a step, stared straight back at Elkridge, and leaned in towards The Demon. "Is he a monk?"

"My associate here --" The Demon started.

"Associate?! But wait, aren't you from a parallel universe or some shit?"

The Demon raised his eyebrows. "Yes. But we have known him for many years. Calm down, Mister Locosa. Elkridge just gave you some power. It may interfere with your personality for a few seconds. Sorry, I really should have warned you about that."

Nigel took some deep breaths. "So about the monk thing...."

"It's a projection." Elkridge explained. "A projection that just so happens to be from a parallel universe."

"But not the Ultra Space one..."

Elkridge looked confused. He started to think about how he could whiteboard this shit out here, where whiteboards are supposedly quite rare.

"Different parallel universe..." The Demon explained. "...and that's all there is to it." He said with a smug satisfaction.

Elkridge smiled . "There is more to space than just the multiverse." The Demon went up to Elkridge, placing his left hand on Elkridge's right shoulder and whispered in his ear. Elkridge then turned his focus to Nigel.

"My dear boy, my associate tells me that you are a talented fighter." Elkridge began.

"Well, growing up in some of the roughest areas of London, I always had to defend myself."

Elkridge skipped a beat. "Indeed. Well, our enemies are a lot more powerful than John the Gangsta from Canning Town whose only real weapons are a small knife and a hard dick. You have to purely outsmart the enemy now, and up here, in this Spiritual Realm, we have just the weapon."

Nigel was taken aback by the old monk's casual use

of such language. He gained his composure relatively quickly, and asked: "...and what weapon would that be?"

Elkridge beckoned him. "Come, follow me. I'll show you." They walked further until they reached a red brick wall and door made of gold. The wall was about five meters across, and it didn't look like it was connected to anything. Nigel was going to say something, but at this point, he really couldn't be bothered.

Elkridge touched the door with his right palm. Again, he smiled. "It'll take just a moment fellas. Took them forever to construct this door. Mostly because they ran out of money half-way through." He laughed quietly. "A half-working quantum door setup. Quite a mess, that was. Trying to keep the "Under Construction" sign from blipping out of existence every other second was an utter pain in the backside."

A white light encased the door, as it disappeared, revealing nothing but darkness. Next to the door, there was a sconce containing a wooden torch. Elkridge grabbed the torch and cautiously, the three men entered.

Nigel started feeling weird. He felt a pain. Except, no. It wasn't a pain. It was much deeper than that. It was like something was trying to burst out of him. But not a thing like in the Alien movies, he realized. No, it was more like a force.

"Argh!" was all he could muster before collapsing towards the floor. The floor was matted, and this fact struck him as strange. The other two men stopped, turned and aided him up. The pain subsided ever so slightly. They continued walking.

"This is the Realm of the Soulless." Elkridge mentioned.

"...But aren't I just a soul right now?"

The Demon felt the need to correct. "No. You are a spirit. You have a soul. You are not a soul."

Nigel looked confused.

"When you died, there is a projection of you, just like our friend Elkridge here, into the Spiritual Realm. Your soul is intact inside this projection."

"So, the pain I had…"

Elkridge interjected. "…it's just your soul trying to escape. It knows what this place is meant to be and knows it does not belong, but don't worry about that." Elkridge flashed Nigel a grin. Nigel's face started losing color.

"Don't worry?! What kind of fucking reassurance is that?! I'm about to lose my fucking soul!"

"I enchanted you earlier when we shook hands. I assure you, your soul is safe."

"Oh, that's a big fucking relief." Nigel replied, the sarcasm dripping from his lips. The pain, however, took one last stab before calming down to reasonable levels. Color returned to his face.

"So why are we here?" Nigel asked.

Elkridge turned and smiled. "Because a place where no souls can normally enter allows us the privacy we need."

They reached a nearby wall. Elkridge placed the torch in a nearby sconce and the room lit up.

Nigel saw that this place was reminiscent of a dungeon. The walls were dark, the floor was obviously padded and upon the wall he saw all sorts of chains, whips, handcuffs, and various sharp implements ranging from small pointy sticks to full-on knives. To Nigel, it looked like any other Thursday night, but he thought it would be wise to keep that to himself. The Demon recognized the look of familiarity on Nigel's face and laughed heartily. He took out a spliff which had "Galactic Smokes" carved into the side of it, put it to his mouth, and snapped his fingers, causing the spliff to light. Behind them, the entrance door materialized.

"Good." Elkridge started. "Now we can start."

"Start what?" Nigel inquired.

"Your test, dear boy." The monk smiled and rubbed his hands together enthusiastically. They glowed red, and he quickly separated them, and pointed his palms at Nigel. A tremendous blast of red energy blasted from Elkridge's palms towards Nigel, who, stupidly and yet smartly at the same time, tried to block it with his hands, whose green aura successfully kept the red blast at bay.

"What the fuck am I doing?" Nigel asked.

"I enchanted you, remember?" Elkridge smiled and sent a red-blue-green fireball Nigel's way. Nigel felt this energy appending to his soul within him. He felt the metal within him soften.

"What the...?"

The Demon nodded towards Elkridge.

"...ah, fuck it!" Nigel exclaimed as he held his palms together, formed a green fireball and threw it in retaliation. As it approached Elkridge's ball, it turned yellow then red, and both balls stopped in midair. Silence dropped, thus giving tension the opportunity to rise into the air and give the impression that it wasn't going to leave without an eviction notice. All of a sudden, Nigel's ball turned green, and both balls crashed into each other, causing the tension to be evicted and causing esoteric signs on the ceiling to light up in bright blue fire. The room appended itself with a corridor, with a bright light at the end. Both men saw it and knew what it meant. They started running down the corridor parallel to one another and flashes of light appeared between them every few seconds as they sent fireballs at each other. Finally they reached the light, which had now, Nigel realized, misdirected them. The light itself was coming from a giant ring of fire on the padded floor.

"How is this possible?" Nigel asked.

Elkridge laughed lightly. "Step into the ring." He did so, and so did Elkridge. Around them, the flames rose to the ceiling. It is at this point that the Demon started to casually make his way down towards them. Towards the end all he saw, all he saw was a mass of yellow then bursts of red, green and occasionally, blue, which was normal behavior once the ring was considered occupied. The Demon at this point, through the haze and influence of recently puffed substances, was suddenly reminded of Christmas, and started humming a carol.

Once the men stepped into the circle and the flames rose, the men stopped with their fireball-swapping. Nigel made a fist and attempted to strike Elkridge in the nose. Elkridge bent his arm and raised it to his face, blocking Nigel's fist with the elbow. This caused the flames to turn blue for a brief second, and an energy ball formed between the men, pushing them back to opposite sides of the ring. The flames then returned to their natural golden glory. Nigel looked frantically at his hands and gave Elkridge the kind of look he'd give to someone who just brutally murdered his dog with a bread knife. He made fists with both hands and clenched, causing green auras around them. Elkridge smiled mischievously as red auras formed around his fists. They ran towards each other, fists making contact in the middle, making a noise like church bells. Then, overhead, a band calling themselves The Training Concerto went into action.

An electric guitar started thrashing chords, and drums boomed to the beat of the punches, as the men went back and forth. Each blocking the other's attack with perfect precision. After a while, the music started to die down, and the band left. So did the flames.

Then the fist auras died down, and the only light source came from two places: the torch on the wall, and the Demon's spliff, which by this point was causing the Demon to trip balls even further down the rabbit hole of highness. He was, however, attempting to keep this under control. He was grinning wildly and was about to suggest they get in the hot tub with Jesus Christ himself, when suddenly Elkridge stomped his right foot upon the padded floor, which despite the aforementioned padding, sounded like a shotgun, snapping the Demon out of his "chilling with Christ" haze.

Nigel tried to catch his breath and patted his body down. "Wait...so...I got my body back? I'm all soft now."

"Side effect of the enchantment." Elkridge explained. "Once it wears off, your spirit will go back to its metal feeling husk. Anyway...on to round two!"

Out of the ground, skeletons appeared -- at least that was what Nigel was thinking at first. But, no, he started to realize that they weren't all completely bone, they had flesh, and rags. Their eyes half-closed. A long frown was on all their faces -- almost zombie-like. He recognized the look. These are the kinds of people he used to bump into on the streets back when he was dealing. Except these people right here had a lot more zest and life to them. They marched (or rather slumped) their way towards Nigel.

"Behold the Zombie Minions of the Realm." Elkridge announced.

The Demon walked over to Nigel. "Now, Nigel, your job is to command that army and turn them against Elkridge."

"Turn a whole army? Against that powerful fucker?! Are you high?"

The Demon sighed slightly. "Well, yes, but that's beside the point. It is your job to do this. Think of it as your destiny. Your ultimate destiny." Then The Demon's voice lowered and became gruffer. "It is your final...destiny..." He then went on to describe destiny in a way that only a high Demon could describe destiny.

"It is....the thing that you do..." He started. "The thing that you were put in this multiverse to do. Or is it the universe? Can you be duplicated Nigel? Nah...not someone special like you...so multiverse then." His voice became slurred slightly but also slightly more excited in tone. "It's like in The Matrix. When Neo became the One, it was destiny." He smiled and nodded at Nigel in a very smug way. "Just as it is yours to turn those minions against that old cunt over there. Remember he is only out to destroy you. So you must destroy him first..." The Demon trailed off. Nigel stepped forward a single step, and as his first foot made contact with the padding, the minions froze. A green aura covered the entirety of Nigel's body. His soul, and thus his brain, knew what was going on. He continued for a few steps, and his aura became brighter and more prominent until he became a walking light, so bright that Elkridge had to shield his eyes. Nigel stopped and clicked his fingers. The minions turned and started marching towards Elkridge. The Demon smiled. "Atta boy." He muttered under his breath, as he went for another puff of his spliff.

Caroline and Thrakus started walking through a park. The grass was still green, the sky was still blue, and fellow squirrels fled in fear at the mere sight of Caroline (word gets around very quickly in the squirrel community). Thrakus noted that all this was perfectly normal; thus, there was still time.

"Caroline, do you believe in aliens?" Thrakus asked.

Caroline laughed. "What are we? Children?" Then she thought for a moment. She thought about what happened at the airport. She remembers meeting Matthew, and the words he said to her. About the parallel universes, about her family trapped in PU 131B, and a single tear fell down her cheek.

"Yes, of course I think aliens exist."

Her one tear then turned into a full-on emotional breakdown after about two seconds. Thrakus held her.

"People who say those without souls lack any sense of emotion are full of bullshit." He whispered into her ear. She smiled, and slowly the faucets from which her tears flowed, switched off. They walked further into the park and found some nearby woods. Caroline motioned towards it. Thrakus was hesitant at first, but then cautiously followed Caroline into the woods.

"What's the matter?" She asked.

"Oh, I was on this Terra-formed planet a while ago. The one rule they had was never to go into the woods, because that's where the bears lived."

"...and the bears ate the people?"

"...no. They raped the people. Remember that children's song about the teddy bear's picnic?"

"Yeah..."

"...well, that originated from this planet...Moscos, it

was called. Except the people there knew what the big surprise waiting for them was. Thus, why the song said to go in disguise. The people of Moscos eventually harnessed the power of illusion and used invisibility to their advantage, but that was well after I left the planet, relatively speaking."

Caroline thought about this for a second. She remembered the impression she got from him when he first arrived at her door. It all made sense now.

"I see." She replied. She didn't make sense of it all though. She had no idea what it was she was about to have to do.

"So, really...." Caroline started "...why are you here?" Thrakus, and in turn, Caroline, stopped. She walked back to him. He took her hand in his and made eye contact.

"I'm sorry for this, I really am, but you're just going to have to listen to this." He leaned in and kissed her on the forehead.

Elkridge snapped his fingers and the minions disappeared in a puff of smoke. He grinned at Nigel.

"Good. Your training is now complete." With that, the men exited the arena, and were beneath the stars once again.

"So, what now?" Nigel asked. The Demon approached him from behind and put his arm on Nigel's shoulder.

The Demon, puffing at his spliff, said nothing. He offered it to Nigel. Nigel puffed, and with an exhale, he spotted that a solitary star went out in the sky.

Marwood walked down the corridor from the entrance to the station. Deep down inside, he was feeling rather nervous. His heart rate was way up, and he was getting the jitters. Being, potentially. the one to end the universe, does things like that to a man.

At the end of the corridor, he reached the giant green door with a keypad lock and entered the code in the keypad. The lock was released, the door opened, and in he went. Around the table sat Dorius at the head. On the left-hand side of the room, relative to the entrance sat General Courtney, with a cigar in his mouth, puffing away like he owned half the universe because he married the creator.

Next to him was Senior Officer Samlore, who looked incredibly nervous, which was perfectly understandable given the circumstances, but that was not the reason why he was nervous--the reason why he was nervous was that he had been recently promoted because the last five senior officers had gone missing in the midst of the war, "details unknown", which again was perfectly understandable given the quantum aspect of the enemies at hand; again, though, this was not the expected reason for their absence. Maybes liked to play games with captured officers, such as "Quantum Hide and Seek," where the officers got so frustrated, they ended up shooting themselves in the head.

Lastly, there was Rodney, who was still coming to terms with everything, but coming through like a trooper, the true military Somerfieldian he was destined to be.

Upon entering, the men stood up and saluted Marwood.

"Rodney has been informed." Dorius stated.

"Thank you, Dorius." Marwood replied, rather hastily.

Senior Officer Samlore turned towards Dorius.

"You know, Dorius...this...holographic universe thing isn't so bad..."

General Courtney turned to Senior Officer Samlore and flashed him the kind of look that accused him of bringing his dog over to the house, and it shitting on the expensive shag carpeting. This actually happened at a party once, except there was no dog, and General Courtney was away (hence the party -- all of the military units knew that the gate code to Courtney's premises was 6969 and was the only place capable of holding such a shindig), leaving the housekeeper to clean it all up. Senior Officer Samlore was slightly distressed by the whole thing, not because he was embarrassed about shitting on the carpet; he just loved shag carpets.

General Courtney made a start on getting up, but Dorius motioned for him to sit back down. "Let the man speak." He said softly.

Samlore sat up -- all eyes were on him. "Well, this new universe...it's a lot bigger in terms of storage. Just think..." He started to trail off "...infinite amounts of shag carpeting--"

General Courtney stood up. "I've heard enough!" burst from his mouth. Samlore's eyes widened for a second, but then he closed his eyes.

Samlore remembered growing up in the Somerfieldian Gardens of Lorean. He was an orphan -- his parents died in a disaster on an interplanetary cruise when he was four years old. He and his sister, Shanwise, were brought up by their aunt. During the summer, they both frolicked in the fields among the harmless playful bees, and stray but friendly dogs. He remembered sipping lemonade on a park bench, with his sister and aunt.

"You are destined for great things." His aunt stated.

"Bollocks. The only thing he'll be good for is mopping up the streets!" Shanwise joked.

"Oi!" He exclaimed and punched her in the arm. She rubbed it. Then she smacked him upside the head and laughed.

"Now, now children! This is a place for peace, remember? Now quiet down before I put you both in the Chamber for timeout."

"Yes, Aunt Mary..." They both replied dutifully.

"Now, Samlore, I see you as very important. You have the capability even, to lead men. Great men. Some may be skeptical of your approach but go with it. Trust your instincts."

Samlore opened his eyes again. He looked General Courtney in the eye.

"General Courtney, with all due respect, I think there is something about this new universe that you would like too."

General Courtney raised an eyebrow and took another puff of his cigar. "...and what would that be, Senior Officer Samlore?"

"General, the shagging there is more than just carpet-- think about all of the conquests one could have..."

"Infinite shagging?" General Courtney rolled his eyes off a bit, thinking about it.

"Well, I mean..." Samwell cleared his throat. "I'm sure there is that aspect, but you could build a bigger army, better defenses. You could live like a king."

General Courtney grunted approvingly.

"Senior Officer Samlore!" Dorius boomed behind him. "Just what are you saying? That we should stop fighting?"

"Well, we are already incognito, partially inside their universe. it wouldn't affect us."

Rodney stood up. "...but what about everywhere else?"

"Well....I mean....they....would be taken over...I...guess."

"Destroyed?"

"...maybe."

Marwood piped up "No, no. Fuck that shit. No one is dying on my goddamn fucking watch!" With that, he actually fiddled with his watch and set a time field on himself, Rodney, and Senior Officer Samlore.

"Senior Officer Samlore, just what the hell are you thinking?!" Marwood asked.

"Well, I was thinking, this whole new universe isn't bad. You know, evolution of the species, change is good, and so is cheese--"

"I'd have to agree with the cheese part." Rodney interrupted.

"No, no no. Not at the price of destroying the universe. Look, Senior Officer Samlore. What is it that you want?"

"Shag carpets. But, like, a lot of it. And with the new universe, I know I can get that."

Marwood took off his sunglasses and made direct eye contact with Samlore.

"Well, then." Marwood said softly, "I'm sure we can come to some kind of arrangement."

Samlore's eyes widened, like he just orgasmed. Marwood patted him on the back.

"Soldier, you are dismissed." Marwood deactivated the time field.

"Right, back to business...and back to the war." Marwood announced.

"Well, now, there was a mention of infinite shagging. Are we really sure we want to go through with this?" General Courtney asked.

"Oh, for God's sake..." Marwood fiddled with his watch again.

The planet of Moscos had changed greatly since the time Thrakus was there. The people and the bears formed a truce in light of the recent universal war. The ground was shaking. The bears in the forests were ready. The people in the command center, who used a soulless tracking instrument to track the quantum beings, gave their signal. The bears channeled their inner animal, formed fireballs from their paws and shot them to the sky, roasting everything in their paths.

CHAPTER 10

WHEN THE UNIVERSE GETS SCREWED - MAYBE. PART 1

The kiss of a popudei has the potential for conveying a lot of information very quickly (unless it is a french kiss, of course). In this particular case, Thrakus kissing Caroline on the forehead conveyed the following information:

"I really don't know what will happen next, but you need to be strong. I have brought with me a very powerful gun, given to me by an ancient master in my time of need. You are to take this and defend the Earth against enemies known as the Maybes, who have come to take the entire universe from all of us. Being soulless, you are one of the very few on this planet (and certainly the only one out of those I can trust) who will be able to perceive them, and thus destroy them. I really do wish you the very best of luck."

With that, Caroline collapsed to the ground, and Thrakus disappeared -- his projection had other places to be. He left a large silver gun, with blue stripes running down it in his wake. As she picked it up, the ground started shaking.

Nigel took a puff of the Demon's spliff. He was sitting

on a couch with Elkridge and the Demon.

"Nigel, have you ever kissed a zombie?" Elkridge asked.

Nigel choked on a puff, passed it to the Demon very quickly.

"Well, I've had a few girlfriends that--" Nigel started.

The Demon laughed heartily. Elkridge giggled his way to the floor.

The Demon fist-bumped the human. "I know what you mean, man...I think...I think we've all been there!"

Then the ground started shaking. And then, the high kicked in.

Once Marwood got everyone back timewise, he turned to Dorius.

"Now, what's the plan?"

"Well, we did get some help from an associate."

Marwood paced towards Dorius and then in small areas reasonably close to him. It helped with the thinking.

"Associate? What kind of associate?"

"A clever one. He helped us with this ship..."

"Ah. I think I can guess."

Dorius gave a puzzled look. "Oh yeah?"

"Yeah, there's only one person I know of that can figure out how to do anything tied to dealing with this new universe -- Mike Danger, the Safety Inspector."

"Yeah, that's the man, rather charming chap...paid him a visit a little while ago. Purely business matters. I had a bad case of the runs though -- you should never eat at a place called Taco Hell after 10pm. But at this point, for me, it's sort of a tradition before visiting the man."

A thought clicked within Marwood. For a minute,

he stood, scrunched his eyes, and examined the old man. Behind all the robes, was there a man with the power to completely destroy toilets throughout the universe? Marwood shook the thought out of his head and attempted to compose himself back to the present. "Anyway, so he has something for us?"

"Yes, he built some apparatus that we can use in any of our battle-crafts." He paused for a second. "It has a soulless nature to it. It can detect these quantum beings."

Rodney laughed. Marwood turned. "What's that about, mate?"

"Well, that'd mean this Mike Danger has provided us with a Deus Ex Machina to all this, hasn't he?"

Marwood grinned, laughed a little, and fist-bumped Rodney.

"I wonder if he took any of that advice..." Rodney started.

"What advice?"

"The nail advice in the magazine he was reading when we were at that weird nightclub with the holograms."

Then Marwood remembered about the daffodils in his last encounter with the man. But with Rodney around, he thought it best to keep this realization to himself. Keep soldiering on.

"Alright then, what are we waiting for, Christmas? Dorius, lead the way!"

...and he did.

In a neighboring galaxy, Christian Lucifer gathered with his armies of Maybes. A Maybe was a small metallic creature with four spikes for legs, and four tentacles, two on their left, two on their right. These tentacles packed one hell of a whack, but also have the capability to act

as highly powerful laser guns. Their eyes are all around
-- to the regular human (if a human ever actually saw
one), they would look like a ring of multi-colored LEDs.
They have a hive nature, trying their best to protect their
own, for the sake of Sophos and the new initiative of the
holographic universe.

"My friends." Christian started. "We are about to
invade the solar system. Now the majority of this will be
easy, but there is one particular spot that we need to pay
attention to -- they may even be aware of our upcoming
invasion of their homeland."

A Maybe was writing notes with a pen in its notebook.
So far, it read: "Solar system - piece of cake except for
one spot. Oh, dear God." He wasn't exactly the most
optimistic soldier in the group, but there are always a few
of those.

"Which place is this?" He asked their great leader.

"It is Sol-3, known to others as Earth. Now, the special
thing to keep in mind is that it has a Tier 1 Underworld,
which contains a lot of infrastructure, including a
spiritual realm."

"You've been there before, haven't you?"

"Yes. Strictly business." He replied, shifting his eyes
slightly. "Anyway, I'll take a few of you with me to the
spiritual realm. The rest of you, take over the actual
planet. That should be easy -- all humans have souls."

"Errr, sir?"

"Yes?"

"Why are you not attacking the Underworld? Isn't
that central to Earth's infrastructure? Destroy that, and it
would all be yours in an instant, surely."

"Because." He paused. A good question from a Maybe.
He was almost proud. "I know a thing or two about about

the Underworld there. It's heavily guarded by Ultra Space monks, and, well, that's a lot of hassle. If we attack the Spiritual Realm, that links down to the machinery in the Underworld, bringing the whole thing crashing down."

The Maybe nodded with approval. Not that Christian Lucifer needed it.

...and everywhere on Earth, the ground shaking became more violent.

CHAPTER 11
WHEN THE UNIVERSE GETS SCREWED - MAYBE. PART 2

Caroline adopted a battle pose. She took the gun with both hands, and held it at the hip level, pointing it up into the sky. By the look of her, one would think that she knew exactly what she was doing. Caroline, however, did not. *I hope you're right, Thrakus.* She thought. A couple of tears dribbled down her cheek. *Not that I care so much of my own wellbeing, but if I survive this, I'm bringing my family home.* And though she thought it was impossible to do so, it was still something to hold on to.

Marwood, Rodney, General Courtney, and Senior Officer Samlore followed Dorius down a number of corridors. Eventually, they reached a door with a golden wheel. Inside the golden wheel, there was a shiny silver number pad with a small screen above it. Dorius typed in a seven digit code and turned the wheel clockwise. At least that was what would have happened if he had been able to turn the wheel, but it was locked because he put in the wrong code. It's times like this, he was thinking that he wished there was just a master key he could use for all of his doors. He started fumbling through his robe.

"Come on Dorius, we don't have all day!" Marwood

exclaimed.

"Yes, with all due respect sir, we might be getting our destruction and infinite shag on a lot sooner if you don't put in the right code!" General Courtney shuffled his hands enthusiastically. Marwood facepalmed himself softly. Finally, Dorius found a scrunched up piece of paper, he opened it up and typed in the digits that were on it. The door opened, and upon the screen it read off: 52 58 1 10. Rodney saw the numbers on the screen, and suddenly felt like he understood a lot more about how the universe worked. He looked to Marwood, who flashed him a grin. They all walked through and were greeted with a battle craft. It was small, with bright red paint. It had room for two people up front in the cockpit, and a small area in the back with two seats. The back seats manned the guns which protruded out to the side of the ship. There were two guns on each side, one above the other, a few feet apart. They were the size of cannons. They were also greeted by Mike Danger. How he got there no one but him knew -- Marwood was the only one who gave any sort of facial reaction to this, but he knew the universe and Mike well enough that it was probably best not to ask but was surprised at the lack of nail decor. They walked right up to the ship. Mike leaned his elbow on the lower left gun.

"So, in this ship, you should be able to track the Maybes, due to some soulless technology I devised on my treks throughout many universes." Mike explained.

"So, these guns..." Marwood said, he paused, and examined the right lower gun. He stroked it softly. "...what do they fire?"

"It's a very powerful laser blast." Mike replied.

"...and that will work, will it?" Rodney asked.

"It should. The material this is made from can obliterate most things in the multiverse. Remember, the Maybe's greatest power is the fact that they cannot be perceived. Hopefully, they won't be ready for us. Now, if you don't mind..." Mike produced a small green tin from a pocket inside his jacket. "I've had enough of this professional speak...y'all up for a safety meeting?"

Inside the Spiritual Realm, the Gang of Three (as they would later be known according to Multidimensional historians) started to prepare. They emerged from the hallway tripping balls. The rumbling and shaking only increased in intensity, causing the Three to be paranoid that the Great Big Green Monster in the Sky had come for them. They huddled together in a close corner, wondering when the sky was going to fall. Above them stood a man with a sword. A man that held the sword in such a manner that he meant business with it. Had Nigel not been on the verge of having a panic attack, he would have immediately recognized the man, and recognized him as being on their side, what with the leather jacket and short haircut et al.

"Get up!" The man boomed in a gruff voice.

"Thrakus?!" Nigel exclaimed.

Thrakus extended an arm down to help Nigel up, and they both helped up Elkridge and the Demon respectively.

"Now, you're going to need this." Thrakus gave Nigel the sword. "...you know what to do with it, and what to do in the case that it fails you.

"Not that it should." He muttered under his breath. "This sword was forged in the Den of Darkness in the Draconian sector of the Universe; may it rest in peace. Now..."

He turned to Elkridge. "You, sir, have betrayed your Order!" He boomed.

Elkridge was too out of it to reply.

"If you get out of this, then fine, you'll get an automatic pardon. But if not, you will get reported to the Multidimensional Paragon. Space Weed is not for monks. especially your kind. You should be ashamed of yourself. Still, I see you all are being a tad bit unresponsive..."

Thrakus reached into his pocket for his shuriken. It was not there.

Drat. He thought, *I'm going to have to do this the old-fashioned way...*

He stretched out both arms and closed his eyes. A bright yellow light encased his palms -- he pointed his palms in the direction of the Three, and instantly, they seemed alive again. Thrakus slumped slightly for a second, exhausted.

"Now fellas." Thrakus took a deep breath. "I have to run." ...and with that, Thrakus disappeared.

The walls started breaking. Instantly, the Three stood back. Elkridge and Nigel closed their eyes and closed their fists. They started chanting a summon prayer. Their fists started glowing, and then they opened their eyes and opened their fists. Armies of Zombie Minions rose from the ground, at the exact point the walls started breaching, letting in a flood of Maybes. The Minions started whacking very powerful swings at the armies. The flooding of Maybes continued, until eventually, emerged Christian Lucifer, with a double-bladed sword in hand. As he walked towards the Three, he waved his hand over the ground, causing the Maybes and Minions to make a path. He, unlike the Maybes, was not surprised at what he saw. It was almost like he sacrificed some of his own children, knowing that they were going to encounter something they weren't prepared for.

"Ah." Christian Lucifer remarked, upon seeing the Three. "Three guardians, eh? No problem." He reached around his back and produced another double-bladed sword. He came at them swinging the sword with his wrists vertically, mockingly.

Elkridge and the Demon came forward with energy blasts, providing a force-field keeping Christian back. They both started to scream like they were in pain; this force-field was taking a lot out of them. Nigel stepped forward, ready. Elkridge and the Demon stopped and stepped back. Elkridge went back to summoning more Minions.

"Now, Mister Locosa." Christian started. "I get to finish what I should have done a while back." He took a swing with his left sword, to which Nigel raised his sword and defended. Christian smiled "Ah, Draconian too? I see." He licked his lips "Well, then...say hello to my other little friend." He took a swing with a sword in his right hand.

"...and say hello to his!" The Demon announced, stopping the swing with his right arm. The blade cut him deep, but it did not deter him. He used all of his Demon strength to push back the right arm, all the while, Nigel was engaged with a sharp discourse with Christian's left sword. Swing, defend, swing, defend. After about six back and forths with this, Nigel's sword hand started to glow, and he saw the pattern. Swing, defend, and then he went in for a stab. Which Christian defended with his other blade. Christian laughed menacingly.

"Not so fast, Mister Locosa!"

At this point, the Demon had totally pushed back

Christian's arm all the way behind his back and held his arm there with all of his Demon strength. His hands started glowing, which kept Christian's right arm firmly behind his back like it had been handcuffed, which allowed him to circle around Christian, and punch him in the face with the spare fist so hard and fast that there was not much opportunity or point to defend. Christian would have staggered back were the Demon not holding him, giving Nigel the chance for a stab in the heart, which he went with a full thrust. Christian coughed up blood and the Demon thrust him down to the floor, his right arm still dripping blood.

Christian laughed maniacally and removed the sword bit by bit from his body.

"Doesn't this fucker ever die?" Nigel asked.

"Oh, what a perceptive question, Mr. Locosa! I do not die by your mere mortal means, because I am not mortal."

At this moment, the Demon smiled. Nigel looked worried.

"This is the end. But the moment has been prepared for!" The Demon exclaimed. "I think, Mr. Lucifer, you forget where you are."

All of a sudden, a bright light appeared, muttered something about losing their family on a plane, and proceeded to melt Christian Lucifer down to a puddle of purple goop.

"Well, that was easy." Nigel remarked. The shaking around them then got even more violent, and the ground beneath them gave way.

Maybes took over the skies of Earth. Most people had no reaction. Some people tripping on LSD hid in their basements and their under-stair cupboards, thinking that they were going to get eaten by a bunch of mini-Cthulhus, but that was perfectly normal. Neither case, however, applied to Caroline, who started blasting lasers into the sky, sniping the Maybes off one by one. This happened for about five seconds, before the Maybes figured out what was going on, and they started hurling their way towards her. Her hands turned a dark grey, and the gun started glowing. When she first got the message from Thrakus, she had wondered how she was going to defend the entire Earth. Now she knew; the gun was going to lead her. It started sending out electromagnetic pulses with the lasers, knocking out neighboring Maybes, before rapidly shooting them. Once she had protected the forest from all Maybes in the area, the gun knew what to do. It led her up -- up, up and away. Upon reaching the upper atmosphere, the gun encased her in an air bubble. They got into space, at which point, Caroline turned towards the Earth, pointing the gun towards it.

"Oh, no!" Was her first thought. A first thought was the only one she got to have though as the gun took over her brain.

"Look, it's ok. It'll be ok." The gun told her brain. "You just need to shoot me, and I'll provide a very specific electromagnetic force-field around the entire Earth , disabling all Maybes, and nothing else."

Before she had a chance to ask why, the gun forced her to shoot at the Earth. The Earth glowed red and then turned back to normal. The gun brought her hurtling back to Earth, back to the exact point of her departure. The gun had a further point to make to her brain. "These Maybes can be activated unless completely destroyed. Despite having no soul, you still carry a lifeforce. The destructive force field that would destroy the Maybes, and any Maybes who come in contact with this planet but keep all other life intact, requires you to utilize your own lifeforce." Caroline wept for a second, before , forcefully, pulling the trigger on the gun, which allowed a green forcefield to push out, across the entire world, dissolving all traces of disabled Maybes. Again, this entire process was invisible to most people, except for the people on LSD. Those people thought Gandalf rode in from outer space on a white horse and spelled away the mini-Cthulhu's that they perceived the Maybes as. These same people applauded simultaneously across the world, and even as remote as the forest was, Caroline could still hear it. Satisfied with a job well done, she collapsed, the last of her lifeforce left her, and the gun faded away.

After the safety meeting, the Army of Four (as they were to be known) hopped into the battle-craft, leaving Dorius and Mike behind to keep monitoring things. Marwood took pilot, whilst Rodney took co-pilot. The other two manned the guns. Once buckled in, Marwood looked at the console. He realized this craft wasn't any normal battle-craft; It was capable of so much more -- it could shift to other places in the universe (using a touchscreen and a handy "Search Nearby" category), and even go invisible. He pulled the grey lever for invisibility, and instantly, the craft was shifted out into space.

They could see the swarm of Maybes, eating up matter and behind them, the creation of new matter automatically taking place.

"Alright, guys, fire!" Rodney ordered.

Samlore looked at the console in front of him. It was a touchscreen interface. There were four buttons: "Fire Upper Gun", "Fire Lower Gun", "Fire Both Guns", and

"Eject Seat". He tapped the "Fire Both Guns" button. After this he was presented with a menu entitled "Fire what?" and his options were "Laser", and "Other Projectile". He selected "Laser" and General Courtney did the same.

The laser, unlike the laser on Caroline's gun, was in the form of a laser guided missile, which could automatically tell the distance between it and the enemy (it had been programmed for a quantum signature), and then disperse over a number of enemies. A few blasts later, and they made a dent in the enemies coming towards them.

"Where are we even at?" Rodney asked.

Marwood went through his interface. "Somewhere near Saturn actually."

"I see. So we're helping defend the Earth..."

Marwood didn't answer. He didn't know for sure now. He noticed enemies coming in from behind. He spun the ship around, and with Senior Officer Samlore and General Courtney still firing away, they made a significant dent in the enemies coming from that direction. Then Marwood noticed something. "Oh."

"What?!" Rodney exclaimed.

"Look at the radar."

Rodney did. Maybes were coming from all directions, and they weren't blind.

Crash. The ship shook.

"Oh shit!" Rodney replied.

Crash. The ship shook again.

"'Oh shit!' indeed, my good friend."

"Well, those guns are huge, maybe they split into others that take care of the entire 360 degrees?"

Marwood navigated through the screens on his interface. All while spinning the ship around in the way a disc jockey spins a vinyl on a turntable in order to attempt to keep the enemies at bay. Thankfully, the ship's shields were still holding, but after about a minute of shooting whilst getting crashed into by oncoming Maybes, Marwood saw that they were at 85% shield strength.

"That'd be a negative. I knew that Mike Danger wasn't to be trusted."

"Do you think he did this intentionally?"

"He's a smart man. Of course he did."

"Well, do we just say our prayers and hope to see each other in Heaven?"

Marwood laughed. "Oh, please!" He scoffed. "We do have another option." He went to his touchscreen interface. He thought for a second. He had seen similar ships before. He pressed the "Shift to place" button. After a few seconds of loading, it gave the options: "Search Nearby", and "Search Far". "Oh, please be there." He muttered to himself as he pressed the "Search Far" button. A warning box came up. "Please turn on your positioning system settings and try again." Marwood muttered something about bloody positioning system settings, went back into the main menu, went to settings and turned it on. Upon selecting "Search Far" this time, they managed to see that...no results found. Marwood banged his fist on the monitor "Dammit."

"Well, I for one welcome our new shaggerific overlords!" Courtney exclaimed. He got out a cigar and lit it in between shots. "But this is still fun. Just like space fishing on a cold day..."

Samlore stayed quiet and concentrated on shooting.

Crash, crash. They were at 69% now.

"Alright." Marwood said. "Fuck this noise." He fiddled

with his watch. But it was too late. No time fields could be applied. They were currently squarely within the Holographic Universe territory.

Crash. Crash. Crash. 46%

Rodney's brain couldn't take it anymore. It went into emergency mode, leaving him oddly calm, and a little bit woozy. "If only we had a piece of string, eh?"

String?! Marwood thought. Bloody ridiculous.

He looked at the radar. Of course.

"Courtney, Samlore, concentrate your fire!" He commanded. "In one direction. Right behind us."

Puff, puff. "Aye, aye, cap'n." Courtney replied as he and Samlore swung their guns around to the back.

"Rodney...look, und..." He looked at Rodney. "No, best I do it. But I still need your help. Press the button when I say so."

Crash. 38%

Marwood opened up a compartment next to his seat. It revealed a big red button. From the cockpit, he pulled the ship in reverse.

Crash. 31%

"Now!"

Rodney struggled to reach down, causing him to fumble twice.

Crash 23%

Rodney managed to pound it on the third try. and they zoomed backwards, Courtney and Samlore were still shooting behind, but even so.

Crash, crash, crash.

"Warning Shields are almost completely depleted."

Crash. The invisibility turned off. But they were still zooming, and in the direction they were going, there were no Maybes, meaning they were back in the old universe.

"What...what...did...we...do?" Rodney asked. His brain's recovery was slow. Steady, but slow.

Marwood smirked, "We bought ourselves some time."

"How?"

"This isn't Maybe territory...at least not yet."

Marwood fiddled with his watch, setting a time field around the ship.

"Alright, that's better..." Marwood breathed a sigh of relief. "Now, for my next trick."

He went to the monitor. and went to the "Search Far" screen again. It was scanning...

"You see ...I managed to hook the watch into the ship's network...and managed to feed the main computer with our current time."

Samlore piped up. "But wait a second. We're in a time field..."

"Exactly. The universe is now our oyster. It can't tell where we are, from a space-time standpoint, so it has no choice but to show us every option." Marwood paused. "Of course, that does mean it'll take a while to retrieve the results..."

"And how long is a while?" Samlore asked.

"About 2455 years, give or take a year and a half."

Sensing a need for a better strategy, Courtney and Samlore discarded their stations at the guns and went towards the cockpit area.

"What we need, gentlemen." Marwood began. "...are some data constraints."

"Data constraints..." Samlore drifted off. Marwood knew he wasn't getting anywhere.

"Courtney!" Marwood boomed, hoping the volume would make everyone pay attention. Courtney looked at Marwood and saluted. "Please empty your pockets."

Courtney did as Marwood ordered. There was a wallet, some very shiny medals, and a small piece of shag carpeting.

Ah ha Marwood thought. Now we're getting somewhere.

"General Courtney, where did you get the piece of carpet?"

Courtney blushed, but Marwood knew. He got it from an adventure with Luciel, one of the many he had over the years. She was a popudei though and made no secret about it. Could it be? He grinned at Courtney.

"What are you grinning about, Marwood?"

"I believe you just showed us our ticket out of here. My watch can tell the origin of certain fabricated objects, such as the small bit of carpet you gave me. We can then feed that information into our computer here and get the results that we need."

Courtney looked a bit disappointed. "What about my medals?"

Marwood scoffed. Then gave Courtney a small smile. "Your medals are well deserved, general." Marwood paused, pushing his glasses down his nose, his grin getting bigger. "But I know you have had relations with a certain popudei…and I know you. Must've been a hell of a burn on your bum."

Courtney chuckled. "Yeah …that was one hell of a weekend."

Marwood scanned the piece of carpet, and immediately, the result came on screen. "PU-77C" Marwood grinned. "Strap in, lads!" He pushed the button.

EPILOGUE
GOING AWAY FOR PLEASURE

Instantly, there was darkness, followed by bright, white light. This blinding whiteness continued for about fifteen seconds, and then it focused itself into a small circular object, yellowing slightly against a solid light blue backdrop. There wasn't a single cloud in the sky. And just as instantly, Rodney jumped out of his mental slump. Blue. Sky. But wait a minute, the last thing I recall was that we were fighting...which can only mean...

"Where are we?" Rodney asked.

"A parallel universe." Marwood replied.

Rodney turned his head to the side, giving a skeptic look. "I'm sorry, I don't understand."

"What we just did...." Marwood said slowly. "...was that we jumped universes."

"You mean we just left it? We just left our universe."

"Yup."

" What about Earth?"

Marwood laughed. He gestured to the window.

"Not what I meant, Marwood."

Marwood stopped laughing and snorted, "Yes, I guessed as much." He said gravely.

"So." Rodney began. "What happened to Earth? My Earth."

"Probably destroyed."

Rodney was speechless. "You're having me on, aren't you?"

Marwood gave Rodney a look. Straight in the eyes.

"Now, Rodney..."

"Oh don't 'Oh Rodney' me. This isn't about a spilled drink or someone's puke on the couch..." At this point, General Courtney burst out laughing. Marwood stared at him and he stopped.

"...that was my home!"

"No, it wasn't." Marwood stated.

Rodney started to get frantic. "It was..." He was groping for words, but was too caught up in a sudden awareness of present events. "It was..." A single tear ran down his face born from the fiery pit of frustration, which in Rodney's case, just suddenly imploded. "It was the only home I ever knew..." He said coldly.

"Rodney, as I always say, I always take care of you..."

Rodney's mind flashbacked to the last time Marwood said this. Sitting on a park bench, on a planet far away from Earth, with the three curious moons. He remembered Marwood saying about how they would end the war.

"Didn't you also say that we were going to end the war?"

"Yes I did."

"Well...didn't we just run away from the war instead of ending it?"

"Our war is still to come."

"...and that is?"

Marwood looked him straight in the eye. "You'll know when the time comes."

"I see. So. What about Caroline?"

Marwood sighed. "I don't know. Maybe Thrakus came for her and took her outside of that universe."

"Can he do that?"

"I don't know. but I hope so."

"Marwood..."

Marwood took off his glasses and stared at Rodney. He didn't want to do it, and he understood; after being through what Marwood had been through during his life, by God he understood what Rodney was going through. But now was not the time for discussion. They had guests. He stared at Rodney for about five seconds, after which, Rodney began to show signs of relaxation. He didn't forget his worries, persay -- Marwood just pushed them to the back of his mind. Rodney sighed, drained.

Marwood focused his attention to the ship's surrounding area. "Seems as good a place as any to land." He said. They landed. "Alright fellas, let's see what we have here." They all disembarked.

They landed in what seemed like the wild west. The streets were lined with saloon bars, banks, and general stores, all cemented in the sand that coated the road. Marwood took a look at his watch -- it was about 5 o'clock in the evening, and it seemed like everyone from all over were making their way to the main saloon bar entitled "The Shagging Donkey".

"Hey, hey!" General Courtney exclaimed. "Looks like my kind of place!"

Rodney thought the name was odd for where he thought he was geographically. "Well, we have had a rough day, so I guess it's a pretty good option for now."

He turned to Marwood. "How are we going to get out of here?" Marwood didn't answer; he just turned to Rodney and grinned, as they all walked along.

What they did not know was that they were being followed. Behind them, keeping themselves rather stealthy, were four horsemen who spoke fluent French.

--

Around Kinky, there was darkness. After what she had been through, she found it quite relaxing, until a sudden thought hit her. Am I dead?

"No, you are not dead." Boomed a voice around her. Oh, thank god. And breathed a sigh of relief.

"Kinkiforous the Forth, you have been summoned. Please come." A light ahead turned on, lighting a pathway. Cautiously, she walked forward.

The light shone upon a throne made of gold. Sat upon a throne was a tall man in a business suit. In his hand, a glass of scotch sloshed from side to side. As Kinky came closer, she recognized him. Vallar, Lord of the Psychic Realm. They looked straight into each other's eyes. She knew now was not the time for lies or fooling around. Even if it was, she never could, to him. He'd know, and the consequences for doing so couldn't bare thinking about.

"Kinkiforous--"

"Kinky will do fine."

"Kinky. Some have said you have done a fine job. All, but myself."

"Sir?"

Valler sipped his scotch. "You almost got yourself killed. Twice."

Kinky nodded. Her head hung low. Vallar put down his scotch and approached her.

His hand swung and slapped her with all his might. "Don't do that again."

"Yes sir."

"But you have impressed the counsel, and they have

given you a new mission."

Kinky looked up, but she dare not smile. Vallar snapped his fingers. Lights came on, and all around them were tall stacks of golden filing cabinets. These contained the records of everything that had occurred in the past in some of the universes. Outside the room, there were many similar ones, together comprising all knowledge from all universes, from the beginning of time to the present moment.

Vallar went over to the cabinet third from the top to his left, opened it, and started shuffling through papers. "Well, you know you're going to have to change, right?"

Kinky nodded and smiled. Psychics have the ability to change species depending on the mission assigned to them. When she first met Marwood, her form was human. She loved being human. Being a gorilla, not so much. The constant hunger for bananas and her outward appearance were not her preference. But for the mission of intercepting Rodney's subconscious, it was necessary.

Vallar found his paper and closed the filing cabinet. He presented the paper to Kinky. In the corner bore the Red Seal of the Psychic Realm. The paper read:

Get Kanthor. By any means necessary.

"But...isn't he in Christian Lucifer's custody?" Kinky asked.

"Nope. Managed to sneak out under the radar."

"Wow, that must have been some sort of psychic ability."

Vallar smiled. Then he continued. "Of course, he isn't one of us, but he is very good, and we need him."

"Need him for what?"

Vallar smirked and tapped his nose. Kinky nodded, turned around, and started walking out.

"Your bag, Kinky. We have given you some tools to use." Vallar shouted after.

Kinky stopped and looked into her bag. She beamed as much as a summer sun on a cloudless day, as she approached the Transformation Chamber. She entered and closed the door behind her. A bulb above the door shone green, and dinged in a similar manner to a microwave.

"Here we go again..." She reached into her bag, finding a slight catharsis as the feeling of touch felt all tingly as she went from gorilla to human. She pulled something out. Inside the bag, there was her money-purse (because even psychics have need of some coin), a screwdriver, an ice cream scooper, a roll of duct tape, and some WD-40. But what she held in her now human hand that had her smiling so bright was none of these. In her hand, she held a pair of pink furry handcuffs.